NANCY WARREN

A POISONOUS REVIEW

THE VAMPIRE BOOK CLUB
BOOK FOUR

Cover Design by Lou Harper of Cover Affairs

ISBN: ebook 978-1-990210-49-5

ISBN: print 978-1-990210-50-1

Ambleside Publishing

INTRODUCTION

Too many cooks spoil the stew!

The Irish stew at O'Brien's pub in Ballydehag is a Friday night favorite—until several people get sick and terrible reviews bubble to the surface on social media. Publican and chef Sean O'Grady is horrified, but when one of his customers dies after eating the stew, he realizes he has more than poisonous reviews to worry about. Was Sean the only one who added ingredients to the simmering pot—or does someone have a taste for murder?

Witch Quinn Callahan has her hands full with some new and disturbing residents of Ballydehag. The fortune-hunting Leprechauns aren't as cute as her childhood cereal led her to imagine. And there are a couple of American visitors staying at the local B&B who look a lot like mobsters. Most important of all—can she find out who has been stirring the pot over at O'Brien's?

This picture-perfect Irish village is hiding dark deeds, and it's up to Quinn and her late-night Vampire Book Club to clear Sean O'Grady's name before someone decides that death needs a second helping.

If you haven't met Rafe Crosyer yet, he's the gorgeous, sexy vampire in *The Vampire Knitting Club* series. You can get his origin story free when you join Nancy's no-spam newsletter at NancyWarrenAuthor.com.

Come join Nancy in her private Facebook group where we talk about books, knitting, pets and life.
www.facebook.com/groups/NancyWarrenKnitwits

A POISONOUS REVIEW

CHAPTER 1

"Have you heard the news, Quinn?" Kathleen McGinnis asked with eyes so bright and full of suppressed excitement that I knew she'd be devastated if I'd already heard whatever she wanted to tell me.

I stopped unpacking the new order of books that had just arrived at The Blarney Tome in Ballydehag, Ireland, where I currently managed the only bookshop in the village.

Before I could ask what the news was, my door opened again.

The second visitor was Karen Tate, another shop owner in town. "Have you heard?" she asked, her expression eager.

Kathleen owned Finnegan's, the local grocery store, and Karen was the proprietor of Granny's Drawers, which sold everything from old clothes and junk to antiques. She also ran Ballydehag's only bed and breakfast. Karen was actually a cousin of mine, but I couldn't tell her that for many reasons.

"What's the news?" I asked.

In a town the size of Ballydehag it doesn't take a lot to get everybody excited. No doubt somebody was getting married, or having a baby, or had been seen in a nearby town with someone they shouldn't be with. I liked gossip as much as the next person, so I waited in anticipation.

"The bakery's finally been rented!" Kathleen said and then settled back to see the result of her revelation.

Karen nodded. "Can you believe it, Quinn? Finally, the bakery's been rented."

Honestly, not since 'Netherfield's been let,' had words sounded so full of import.

"That's great," I said, trying to sound sufficiently excited. In fact, it would be very nice to get some good, freshly-baked bread again.

Kathleen did her best bringing in the kind of bread already packaged in bags that every grocery store has, but the bakery that had been operating when I'd first arrived in Ballydehag had produced outstanding loaves, and we hadn't had any since it closed under very unfortunate circumstances. I supposed not a lot of bakers wanted to ply their trade in a town as small as ours. There wasn't a lot of scope for expansion. Still, if you wanted a nice quiet life in a pretty and very traditional Irish village, you could do a lot worse. I hoped the new baker wouldn't be too sensitive to things like witches wandering the main street or vampires living in the local castle. So long as they were sufficiently oblivious to the supernatural, the new people could be very happy here.

"Don't you want to know who's rented it?" Kathleen asked.

"You're obviously dying to tell me, and I have no objection to hearing it," I replied. I really had to stop doing this, as now I was channeling Austen. Still, I couldn't help but hope that the bakery would be taken over by a handsome bachelor.

Though with my luck, he'd be a Wickham, not a Darcy. Maybe I should concentrate on being grateful for fresh bread.

"Well, his name is Paddy McGrath. I only saw him out the window. A nicely dressed gentleman, wearing a proper jacket and tie. Seemed very pleasant."

"Is he single?" Karen asked.

She and I were two of the only middle-aged, single women in town and, frankly, the pickings were slim. Apart from Dr. Andrew Milsom, who I suspected had come here to get away from a woman, though he said it was to enjoy the fishing, there weren't many appropriate unattached men. Of course, most of my social life, if you could call it that, came from my undead book club. Since I was a witch myself, I was perfectly happy to mingle with other supernatural creatures, though they weren't without their challenges.

I wasn't as blatantly curious as Karen, but I was certainly interested in the answer. Was this Paddy McGrath unmarried? It would certainly be nice to have more single men in the community. It would be nice, for instance, to be able to go out for dinner with one. Vampires make very poor dining companions.

"I couldn't say. Bakeries are usually run by families, though, aren't they?" Kathleen shrugged, then said somewhat regretfully, "Besides, he wasn't very tall. Pleasant of countenance, but a little lacking in the height department."

Karen and I glanced at each other, but neither of us said anything. We'd have to make our own evaluations of Mr. Paddy McGrath.

Karen said, "Shall we go to the pub for dinner tonight to celebrate?"

I thought this was taking things a bit far. "You want to celebrate that somebody's taking over the bakery?"

"No, silly. It's Friday. We usually celebrate the end of the week."

This was true. We often had dinner together at the pub on Friday night. I don't know that we were celebrating the end of the week, since both of us had our shops open on Saturdays, but it had become a pleasant routine. I nodded and turned to Kathleen. "Would you care to join us?"

"Well, I won't stay for dinner, but I'd be happy to join you in a drink." That sounded perfect. Kathleen held my gaze. "And we're still on for the foraging tomorrow?"

I was surprised she'd mentioned it in front of Karen. Kathleen had promised to show me some of the more interesting herbs and even some mushrooms that would be useful in my spells and tonics. I had come from Seattle where the climate was similar but not exactly the same. Things like soil and the kinds of trees and weather always affected how things grew. I knew there were plants growing here that I had no knowledge of.

Kathleen, a pretty good witch herself, would be a good teacher. But Karen wasn't a witch. If she came along, what were we going to do? Harvest edible mushrooms?

Fortunately, Karen shook her head with a laugh. "I can't imagine anything worse than digging in the dirt on my hands and knees. Besides, I've got a busy weekend." She couldn't quite keep the pride out of her voice. "The bed and breakfast is full. Every room taken. That's the second weekend in a row that's happened."

"That's fantastic," I cried out. I couldn't be more pleased for her. She'd taken a huge risk, invested everything she had in turning the big, old house she'd inherited into a quality bed and breakfast. There were some challenges, of course, one of them being that Ballydehag wasn't a huge tourist center, the other being that my ancestor, Biddy O'Donnell, an evil old witch who'd been hanged for her crimes and refused to stay dead, had taken up residence in the home since she'd formerly had a property on that very site. Biddy was a big problem in my life. She was also family, which made it difficult to get rid of her.

Karen left, saying she'd see us both later at the pub.

When the door closed behind her, I turned to Kathleen. "What were you thinking, inviting Karen along?"

"If I didn't, she might have been suspicious. And I knew she'd never say yes. The only time Karen Tate gets her hands dirty is if she's cleaning up an old antique of hers. You won't find her in the garden digging in the muck. Don't worry, I know this village and most of the people in it. Even those who live outside of it. If they don't come into my shop to buy their food, I usually deliver it to them. There's not much in Ballydehag I don't know about, Quinn."

She said it almost like a warning. I suddenly had to search my conscience. Was there something I was doing that was going to get me into trouble?

My only big secret was running a very late-night book club for vampires. While Kathleen might not know about the book club, she certainly knew about the vampires. The local witches and vampires operated on a live and let live policy. Apart from the obvious differences between us, we seemed to co-exist fairly peacefully.

In fact, I had to say, if Lochlan Balfour hadn't been a 700-year-old vampire, I'd have found him very interesting. He was tall and gorgeous, and would no doubt show up on one of those lists of the richest people in the world if he wasn't so successfully secretive about his holdings. He ran a high-tech communications and security company with offices all over the world, though he tended to spend as much time as possible here in Ballydehag. I think he liked the weather here. And the castle he owned. As castles went, his was pretty awesome. The only other secret I had from Kathleen was that I sometimes communicated with the woman who'd had this shop before me. Lucinda had left a scrying mirror behind so I could always reach her.

"We've a busy morning, so don't drink too much tonight, Quinn. Or stay out too late."

I nodded, unsurprised at her advice. Kathleen always treated me like I was a brand-new witch, forgetting that I'd been casting spells and brewing potions for twenty-five years. I was new to Ireland, but not to the craft. Still, I knew she'd have things to show me, and I was always open to learning new things.

CHAPTER 2

I was lucky, or I suppose that's one way of looking at it, that I had more than one vampire who was happy to be my shop assistant when I needed a break from The Blarney Tome. The one I liked best was Dierdre. Oscar Wilde called her *dreary Dierdre*, which was very unkind. Dierdre was a Scottish vampire, certainly not as colorful as Oscar, or that reckless kleptomaniac Thomas Blood, or even my not remotely dear—and wish like hell she was departed —ancestor Biddy O'Donnell. Dierdre was polite and, unlike most of the vampires around Ballydehag, not anxious to draw attention to herself. She wore timeless Chanel suits, tweeds, and sensible shoes. In fact, she was exactly the kind of person you wanted as an assistant in your bookshop. She was incredibly well-read, as, in fairness, were most of the vampires. They had a lot of time to read.

She was never going to be the person I called if I set up a summer book fair outside, but since that was unlikely to happen, I wasn't too worried. Dierdre liked the bookstore as much as I enjoyed having her and often came by for a couple of hours in the day to help. I was not one to turn down free labor.

I knew she enjoyed working in the shop, but she also needed her sleep, so I tried not to ask for her help too often. She'd already agreed to take over the shop this Saturday when I'd be foraging with Kathleen, so I was surprised but pleased when she showed up around eleven o'clock that morning asking if I'd like some help.

"I was sleepless and wanted something to ease my mind. What would you recommend, Quinn?"

Since she probably knew the stock of my bookstore better than I did myself, I suspected she only wanted to chat for a few minutes. I was glad to get her advice, as we had to choose a new novel for the vampire book club.

The choosing of a book for the vampire book club wasn't easy. The vampires tended to shun new releases and preferred to discuss the classics. I often thought that was because it was a trip down memory lane for them. We could read about Victorian times, or medieval times, or Elizabethan times, and someone would have an anecdote about something that had happened then. Or they'd be able to tell how realistic a portrait of the time the author was painting.

However, we had an added complication. Since we had put a lot of effort into the recently deceased Bartholomew Branson's launch of his posthumous novel, and even read one of his thrillers in our book club, Oscar Wilde's nose was so far out of joint it was hardly on his face anymore. He wandered around heaving great, long sighs and despairing of modern taste.

"What do you think about us reading *The Picture of Dorian*

Gray?" I quietly suggested to Dierdre, who was both kind and biddable.

This was Oscar Wilde's only novel, as far as I knew. For one thing, I hadn't read it for years. And for another, a grumpy Oscar Wilde was not someone I wanted to spend a lot of time with. When he was pleased and feeling at his best, he was a witty and brilliant companion. Sarcastic, yes. Biting, yes. Occasionally cruel? Most definitely. But a conversation with him was pretty much a joy to anyone who loved wit, cleverness, and wordplay. However, when he was displeased, or his monstrous ego was hurting, he could be a huge pain in the behind. I thought if we flattered him by discussing his famous novel, that might cheer him up.

Dierdre, who had to spend a lot more time with Oscar than I did because they lived in the same castle, was quick to agree. "That's a wonderful idea, Quinn. How kind of you to think of it. That'll put him in a better mood."

I rolled my eyes. "I hope so. You don't think it's too obvious that we're choosing Dorian Gray mainly to flatter him and improve his mood?"

Dierdre gave the matter some thought. "I honestly don't think he'd mind about that. We read Bartholomew's novel, and you launched his posthumous novel in fine style. That's hurt Oscar's feelings. You know how jealous they are of each other. No. If we choose to read *The Picture of Dorian Gray*, I believe Oscar will be delighted."

"Can you suggest it? If the idea comes from me, he might get suspicious."

"Of course. I'll do it today." She paused for a moment. "And I'll have a quiet word with Lochlan, too. If he supports our choice, the others are more likely to go along with it."

I knew she was right. Oscar's biting wit had made him some enemies among the vampires, but everyone respected Lochlan's opinion. I knew he could swing the vote.

"Good, I'll bring in extra copies. Maybe I'll even do a window display of his works." If I was going to suck up to the dead egotist, I might as well go all the way.

The Picture of Dorian Gray, as every Oscar Wilde fan knows, was about a beautiful, young man who made a kind of deal with the devil whereby he remained young and beautiful even as the years rolled by. Meanwhile, his every cruel and thoughtless act was reflected in the face of his portrait, which he kept carefully hidden. I was fuzzy on the rest of the details. I'd have to re-read the classic.

Dierdre was enthusiastic about the book selection. "While I'm here anyway, why don't you go and get yourself a coffee, dear? You look like you could use a break. I'm sure you've at least two copies of *The Picture of Dorian Gray* right here in the store. Perhaps another in the large print section. I'll see if I can find some more."

I didn't really need a break, but I was never one to turn down a chance to get some air. I had a tiny kitchen at the back of my shop where I could make my own coffee, but I preferred going down the street to the local coffee shop and picking something up. I thanked her, grabbed my purse, and left. I'd lived in Ballydehag for a while, but I have to say the high street of Ballydehag is as pretty as any postcard you'll ever find of a quaint Irish village. It is literally like walking back in time. And I took pleasure in it every time I came out here. I still missed things about Seattle. I missed my old friends, my coven, and there was a certain excitement about living in a big city that you'll never get anywhere else. But there's also something about a small Irish village that you'll never get anywhere else. I'd come to love my adopted home, even if it hadn't been my idea to come here.

I might have mused on like this endlessly had I not heard sounds coming from the bakery that still had the sign O'Connor's Bread and Buns in green and yellow hanging over it. Lights were on and I heard a tapping sound, like someone putting up shelves, as I walked by. I was as curious as the next witch, so I decided the polite thing to do would be to introduce myself to the new owner. Therefore, I knocked on the door and turned the handle. It wasn't locked, which I took as an invitation. I entered and immediately heard muttering in the pauses of tapping. There's the kind of muttering that's a person talking to themselves, and then there's the kind of muttering like what we witches do when we're casting a spell. This was somewhere between the two. I didn't sense I was in the presence of another witch, but I didn't feel like this was a regular guy talking to himself, either.

I yelled out, "Hello?"

The muttering immediately stopped. As did the tapping. A little man came out from the back. "We're not open, mistress."

I gave him a big smile. "I know. I'm Quinn Callahan. I run The Blarney Tome bookstore across the street."

Kathleen had been right when she said he wasn't a tall man. Paddy McGrath was barely five feet tall. He wore black trousers and a tweed jacket with a tie. He appeared to be in his fifties, with twinkling dark eyes and curly hair. Maybe his outfit was strange for somebody who was clearly doing some construction, but in the range of my experience, this behavior barely touched the borders of odd.

There was a silence, and then I asked, “Are you a baker?” Maybe it was a stupid question, but he didn’t resemble any baker I’d ever seen before.

He chuckled at that. “Actually, baking will be a new trade for the missus and me,” Paddy admitted. “But I hope we can impress you with our skills, Miss Callahan.” He had an engaging manner, and I smiled back.

“I hope so too. And please, call me Quinn.”

“In fact, it’s my wife who’ll do the baking. I’ll do the managing and no doubt she’ll have me in the front of the shop selling loaves and cakes.”

“You’re going to do cakes?” This was good news.

He chuckled again. “I sense you’ve a sweet tooth on you, Quinn Callahan.”

“If you can make a decent chocolate brownie, I’ll be your customer for life.”

“I’ll have a word with the missus,” he said.

“I won’t keep you, then. But welcome.” I left, thinking life in Ballydehag had just become even more interesting.

Who was Paddy McGrath? And why was he really here?

CHAPTER 3

Kathleen and I arrived at the pub at the same time and so walked in together. I glanced around and there were the usual people I often saw there on a Friday. Well, some of them were no doubt there any day of the week. Danny, the older man who sometimes helped Kathleen in her grocery store, was doing a good job holding up the bar. He was drinking a Guinness, and I suspected it wasn't his first from the vague expression in his eyes and the high color in his cheeks.

Giles Murray, the local photographer, was sitting in a secluded corner with Beatrice, his much younger and very beautiful girlfriend. Giles was a good photographer, and he sold his work all over the world. I was always surprised that he'd chosen to settle in such a remote corner of Ireland. No doubt he worried that in a bigger city he might not be remarkable, or able to keep such a tight hold on his hot girlfriend. She seemed perfectly content, though, sitting beside him drinking what looked like a gin and tonic but could have been a lemonade, for all I knew. Giles had a whiskey, and both of them were busy with their phones.

"Whisht, Giles Murray," Kathleen said, as we went by their table. "What are you doing messing about on your phone when you've a beautiful woman to entertain?"

Giles glanced up, both startled and sheepish. "It's my Instagram account. I have to stay on top of social media. Especially with my new book coming out." I could hear the pride in his tone.

Kathleen immediately went from scolding to thrilled. "Oh, and how's it coming?"

Giles had been boasting about his coffee-table book for so long I'd stopped listening. Kathleen was clearly more supportive.

"Oh, it's grand. The editors were particularly pleased that I captured so many unique characters. I'm chronicling an Ireland that's rapidly disappearing," he said, in a tone that made me suspect he was reciting his own back cover copy.

"Here." He held out his phone so we could see.

On the small screen was a photograph of Danny, the seventy-something resident of Ballydehag who, as far as I knew, had been born here, lived all his life here, and would no doubt die here. In Giles's photograph, Danny was sitting in this very pub, in his usual seat at the bar, with a whiskey in front of him. Such a cliché, except Danny was here right now, having swapped the whiskey for a Guinness.

"Can you see how many comments I've got? And hundreds of likes. Course, that's not the photograph that will be in the book itself. It's one of the many I took when Danny sat for me."

"And isn't that a fine thing? Danny's as pleased as punch

that you included his portrait. Quite a swelled head he's got over it." Was there a slightly questioning tone in Kathleen's voice? Maybe Giles hadn't asked her to be in his book.

Giles must have picked up on it too, for he said, "I really wanted the craggy, characterful faces in my book, not the local beauties like you and Quinn."

"Oh, get away with you," she said, laughing. "A beauty, indeed." But she looked awfully pleased by the compliment.

"The publisher has me working with a publicity person and they really encourage social media. I've never spent so much time on Instagram. Still, it seems to be paying off. I've twenty thousand followers around the world. If they all buy my book, I could have a bestseller on my hands."

I could have told him how likely that was, but he'd discover the tough realities of the publishing business soon enough.

Kathleen and I continued toward a table against a wall that was a couple of tables away from anyone else. Along the way, she greeted those she knew. Since she knew everyone, it was slow going. I didn't know if she knew this, but Karen and I considered this 'our' table as we always sat here if it was vacant. Not for any particular reason except that it was easy to see from the door and it had become a habit. I had a feeling that a lot of the other locals thought of it as our table too because it was amazing how often it was free when we arrived, as it was now.

"What can I get you?" Kathleen asked me.

I knew the pub's menu probably as well as Danny did. I asked for a glass of the Malbec. Kathleen returned holding my wine and a whiskey for herself. I have tried and tried to get on with Irish whiskey, but it's really not my brew.

"*Sláinte*," she said, raising her glass.

I returned the salute, and we both sipped. Andrew Milsom came into the pub, then he seemed to hesitate, and I thought he might come toward us. Instead, he nodded at me and held up the fishing book he'd bought at my shop earlier that day. Then he went to the bar to sit beside Danny.

"I'd say he likes the look of you, that one," Kathleen said.

I leaned closer. "Don't let Karen hear you say that. I think she has her eye on him herself."

Kathleen shook her head. "Andrew Milsom never collected fishing books until you came along. I suspect he reads about fishing a lot more than he puts a rod in the water. It's an excuse to spend time with you, you daft girl."

"Well, if coming into The Blarney Tome to buy fishing books is his idea of a courtship, it's moving at glacial slowness."

She glanced at him, then back at me. "That's an Englishman for you."

Before I could argue against the unfair depiction of Englishmen, the very Irish, very young, and very cute bar owner came over. Sean O'Grady had curly black hair, piercing blue eyes, and a cheeky grin. "You two are a sight for sore eyes," he said with a wink. "Quinn, when are you going to make me the luckiest man in Ireland and run away with me?"

Okay, there wasn't much point defending Englishmen now. There was an undeniable charm about an Irishman. I made some laughing comment, and he continued on his way, delivering two bowls of delectable-looking Irish stew.

I said to Kathleen, "Are you sure you won't stay and have dinner with me and Karen?"

"No thanks, love. I wouldn't want to upset little Bridget."

"Little Bridget?"

"Aye. My cousin's daughter. I helped her get the job here in the pub as kitchen help. It would throw her terribly to think I was going to eat food she'd helped prepare."

I doubted that little Bridget was going to spend a lot of time checking out who was eating, but presumably Kathleen knew her own family better than I did. We talked a little more about the next day's foraging and she reminded me to bring rubber gloves for the nettles. Nettles have a nasty sting in them if you so much as brush past their leaves, but they make an excellent tea, and the plant itself is said to have lots of medicinal properties.

"Also bring knee pads, if you have them. I have gardening ones. They do save the old bones."

I made a note to check the shed and see if Lucinda had owned such a thing.

Karen arrived then. Unlike Kathleen and me, she'd obviously gone home and changed after work. She'd swapped her gray trousers and blue sweater for a pretty dress that I suspected was new, as I'd never seen it before. She'd also taken some pains with her makeup. I was a bit surprised because we saw the same people here every week. And I had a strong feeling she wasn't dressing up for me. She didn't even glance at Andrew Milsom, so presumably this effort wasn't for him, either. She took the third seat at the table beside Kathleen and leaned forward. "You'll never guess what."

She looked too happy for it to be some new horrible event that had happened in her bed and breakfast, so I relaxed. At least Biddy O'Donnell wasn't up to her next dreadful trick I would have to sort out. Luckily, even though Biddy O'Donnell haunted O'Donnell House, Karen was oblivious. Not only was she not a witch, she was completely oblivious to paranormal goings-on. Probably just as well, since she had to live in the bed and breakfast. But how did she never acknowledge that all the televisions switching to The Antiques Roadshow wasn't a normal occurrence? Biddy was obsessed with the show, and had most unfortunately recently set up in business with the notorious thief Thomas Blood, who had once stolen the Crown Jewels in the 1600s and was now a boisterous and unpredictable vampire.

I dreaded to think what was going to happen to the antique market worldwide once those two actually got going. Luckily, so far, there had been unexplained problems with the website—thank you, Lochlan Balfour—and paperwork tended to disappear. Not that it had stopped the pair from amassing a hoard of antiques to sell. Though that hoard did tend to get depleted whenever I heard of something that had mysteriously gone missing. Then I'd make them give back the stolen item.

However, the pair had a real instinct and really did find treasures in junk shops and overlooked attics and barns. It helped that they'd been alive hundreds and hundreds of years ago, so they legitimately knew when something was genuine, but they also had a good sense of style and antiquity. Even I'd seen a few things I wouldn't mind owning except that I refused to support their business on principle. I didn't want it to be a success! My dearest wish was that Biddy and Blood had never begun.

But Karen hadn't come to talk about missing valuables or televisions acting strangely. She said with a pleased smile, "I've got two American men staying with me." She looked at us significantly. "They're in separate rooms, and one was being quite flirtatious with me earlier."

Now I understood the new dress and the makeup.

She said, with false breeziness, "I suggested they might like to experience a proper Irish pub tonight."

I had to admit I was slightly interested. We didn't get many Americans in Ballydehag. It wasn't exactly on the tourist route. Apart from Bartholomew Branson, who was both irritating and undead, I rarely heard another American voice.

"Where are they from?"

She wrinkled her nose. "New York, I think."

"Easterners." I was from Seattle. It was as far from New York as Dublin was from Dubai.

Kathleen, having finished her drink, said, "Well, that'll be nice for you two. What'll you have to drink, Karen? I'll give Sean the order and then I'll head out through the kitchen. I should say hello to little Bridget."

"Thanks. I'll have a glass of red wine too."

Kathleen went off, and we settled in to gossip. I liked Karen a lot. She was good fun, also single, and about my own age of mid-forties. Neither of us were looking for a baby daddy or trying to figure out what to do for a career. I found it a nice stage of life. Of course, I did have the extra complication of magic powers, but even though Karen didn't, we still had quite a lot in common. I suspected that deep down we both were open to another relationship. Maybe. She certainly was, given the way she'd gussied herself up for a couple of guys who were only in town for a few nights.

I said to her, "You do know that New York is about an eight-hour flight from here?"

She waved that away. “One of them has an Irish name. He said how much he likes Irish women.”

That sounded like a pretty bad line to me. “Is he planning to stay, then?”

She shrugged. “I got the feeling that their plans were up in the air.”

“Did they say why they’re here?” It was odd for two single American men to turn up in Ballydehag, of all places. “Is there some sports event I don’t know about? Or a convention?”

“They said they had business in the area. It’s not for me to pry. So long as their credit cards don’t get refused, I’m happy to have them.”

I perfectly understood. She hadn’t had the bed and breakfast going for that long and she’d put every cent she had into it. “Well, let’s hope they have lots of other business contacts and friends and family, and they tell everybody that O’Donnell House is the best bed and breakfast in Ireland.”

She grinned at me. As Kathleen had just handed her a glass of wine, she raised it and said, “And I’ll drink to that.”

Kathleen waved and went off in the direction of the kitchen. I turned to wave and saw a short, plump woman in a white apron slip down the corridor that led to the kitchen. No wonder they called her little Bridget. She was probably about four feet ten inches, but I’d somehow imagined her being a young woman. This gal looked closer to middle age.

Kathleen, of course, stopped to chat and was probably five or ten minutes behind little Bridget before she, too, disappeared into the kitchen.

Karen and I continued chatting, and we’d nearly finished our wine when she said, “There they are.” It was no surprise that she had spotted the two men the second they walked in, as she'd been surreptitiously glancing toward the door ever since she'd sat down.

The two New Yorkers stood side by side, looking around the pub. They were certainly different from the usual clientele.

She said, in a low voice, "That's Billy on the right. He's the one who flirted with me."

I was glad to hear it. The guy on the left was somebody who wouldn't be out of place in a boxing ring. He was completely bald, and not the most attractive guy in the room. His nose had been broken so many times it dominated his face, like a small baked potato. Karen's flirter was definitely the handsomer of the two, not that that was saying a lot. Billy was tall and, while a lot leaner than his buddy, looked like he spent all of his spare time in the gym, too. They both wore jeans, boots, and sports jackets over white shirts. Billy wore his black hair slicked back. When his gaze landed on Karen, he gave her a toothy grin and walked forward. His friend followed a step behind.

"How you ladies doing tonight?" he asked.

I suppose it was the American version of what Sean had said to us earlier.

"Billy, you made it," Karen said, looking delighted to see him. "Do you want to join us for dinner?"

"Don't mind if we do." Billy seemed as assured that they'd be welcome as Karen seemed certain that I would want to have dinner with two complete strangers. I shifted my chair closer to the wall to make room for the big bruiser guy who had no place else to sit but beside me since Billy had already taken the seat beside Karen.

Karen introduced us and then said, "Quinn's American, too."

Billy squinted at me. "Oh yeah? Where you from?"

"Seattle. You?" Not that I needed to ask. Even if Karen hadn't already told me they'd come from New York, their accents gave them away. They sounded like taxi drivers from the Bronx.

He said, "I'm from Queens. Jimmy here, he's from Flatbush. Good to meet another American."

"It's good to meet you, too," I said.

"Let me get you girls another drink." Billy raised his hand and yelled, "Waiter."

Even Karen seemed a little embarrassed at that behavior. "In Ireland, you go up to the bar and order," she said.

He looked unabashed. "My mistake."

He went to the bar and soon returned with two pints of lager and a bottle of the Malbec. It was generous, sure, but I didn't want to have a thick head for foraging tomorrow. Still, if I couldn't brew up a remedy for a hangover, I wasn't much of a witch, was I?

He poured the wine with gusto so the level was near the top of the glasses, and then he settled down with his pint. "I'm hungry. What's good here?"

The other guy finally spoke. "They got Irish stew? I always wanted to have Irish stew in Ireland. My ma used to make it."

"Is she Irish?"

"No. Italian. Don't think her Irish stew was very authentic. I want to try the real thing."

Billy said, "Yeah, sounds good." Then he gestured to us. "What about you girls?"

I tried not to let the word girls grate on me. Not only had

it been a long time since anyone had called me a girl, but where had the guy been for the last twenty years?

Karen, however, was lapping it up. "I'll just have the dinner salad." She gave a giggle I'd never heard her give before. "I'm watching my figure."

Billy gave her a once-over. "So am I."

Oh, I did not know how I was going to get through dinner with these two. "I'll have the salad too," I said in a tone that forbade any cutesy comebacks.

"Do I gotta go to the bar and order dinner as well?" Billy asked.

"I'm afraid so."

"Don't get much service around here, do you?"

Karen shrugged helplessly. "It's just the way it's done here, that's all."

When Billy returned from giving his order, he sat down and his jacket swung forward and hit the table with a low thud. I glanced at him sharply, and he patted his belly. "Cigarette case. Terrible habit. Gotta give it up."

There was a pause before I said, "Karen said you're here on business. What line of work are you in?" It seemed an innocuous enough topic of conversation, and besides, no doubt Karen wanted to know what a guy she was shamelessly flirting with did for a living.

He shrugged. "Just business. Boring stuff," he said. "Jimmy the Nose here," then he gave a short laugh. "Bet you can guess why they call him Jimmy the Nose."

Jimmy glared at his friend. "And no surprise why they call you Billy the Mouth."

Billy turned to me. "So, what do you do? I know Karen runs Ireland's greatest B&B, but how about you, Quinn?"

At least he remembered my name. "I manage the only bookstore in town."

He shook his head at that. "Never been a great reader. Used to like comic books when I was a kid. You read much, Jimmy?"

"The obituaries."

Okay, this was fun. I wondered how soon I could get out of here. Fortunately, our food arrived at that moment. My plan was to eat as quickly as I could and leave. The two men frowned at the substantial bowls of Irish stew mounded with chunks of potatoes and lamb—and generous helpings of bread, too.

"Thanks, honey," Billy said to the waitress. "But you gotta get right back to the kitchen and tell them that me and my friend need two more bowls of this, just like it. And bring more bread."

"But you haven't even tasted it yet," Karen said, sounding shocked.

"Don't matter. Me and Jimmy, we've got big appetites."

I was impressed with the speed at which the two men put away their hefty bowls of Irish stew. I hung on a little longer, curious to see whether they could actually finish the second bowl. Amazingly, not only did they wipe the bowls clean with the last of the bread, but they both ordered dessert. Karen suggested that she and I share sticky toffee pudding, but I'd really had enough by this time. I reminded her that I was going foraging the next day and had an early start. The two men stood when I left and I was slightly embarrassed to find that Billy refused my offer to pay for my dinner. He pulled out a wad of euros.

"I got all this funny money, and I don't know what I'm gonna do with it," he said.

I bade them goodnight and headed out. It wasn't raining, so I decided to walk home.

As I was strolling down the high street, a voice said quietly, "Nice evening?"

I'd long ago learned not to jump when I was spoken to in the dark. "Hello, Lochlan." Had it been nice? Interesting, certainly. I wasn't sure I should tell a vampire that I was pretty sure the man I'd shared dinner with was carrying a gun.

CHAPTER 4

I was up early and excited about a day out foraging. It was a fine autumn morning. When I got downstairs, Cerridwen, my black cat familiar, was already sitting by her bowl, and I told her about my prospective day as I put food in her bowl and refreshed her water. She glanced up at me, looking very unimpressed. She preferred the times when the two of us sat inside a magic circle weaving spells. Potions were of little interest to her since I made them on my own.

"Okay," I promised. "We'll do a magic circle soon."

She sniffed and made a production of crunching her kibble.

As per Kathleen's instructions, I packed a sturdy pair of rubber gloves, as well as secateurs and some old gardening knee pads I found in the potting shed. They smelled slightly of mold, but I was only going foraging so I added them to my foraging bag along with a bottle of water and a thermos of coffee.

My phone rang and, expecting it to be Kathleen, I was surprised to see the caller was Karen. I picked it up immediately and while I'd expected her to tell me how her evening had ended, instead she sounded mildly panicked.

"Are you all right, Quinn?"

"I'm fine. Why wouldn't I be?"

"Jimmy and Billy have been violently ill all night."

"Yuck."

"I checked with Sean O'Grady, and he's in a terrible state. He's had a bad review on his restaurant website. Somebody claiming his food made them sick."

That was never good. Once those reviews were posted, they never came down. "Oh, no. Do you think one of your guests wrote the review?" I hadn't warmed to the two men who'd shared our table last night, but they hadn't seemed like the type to post reviews. Frankly, I doubted they had the English skills.

"They were too sick to hold a pen, never mind type a review on a website."

I took a moment to assess my current state of health, but apart from a very slight headache that I suspected had more to do with the red wine than food, I felt fine. I said, "They didn't keep drinking, did they?" It wasn't only food that made people sick.

"No. Well, I don't think so. After they drove me back to the bed and breakfast, they left again."

"How long were they gone?" I thought about it. "I mean, was it long enough to get blind drunk?"

"I don't think so. It was only about an hour."

"And you feel all right?"

"Yes. Except that I'm worried. I don't want my guests to give my B&B a bad review just because they got sick in my town."

"I'm sure they won't do that."

I opened my cupboard where I kept a stash of various herbs, tinctures, and teas. "I've got a tonic that will help settle their stomachs. It's an old family recipe." I'd found the words 'old family recipe' very useful in giving my brews to non-magic people. I suppose they thought if it had worked for my grandmother, it must be all right. Besides, it also saved me having to recite all the ingredients. "Shall I drop it around?"

"Oh, that would be amazing if you would." Then she wailed, "And the weekend started out so promising!"

I sent Kathleen a message telling her to pick me up a little later than planned and pulled together a tonic, adding some extra healing magic by reciting a spell as I brewed. Then I drove to Karen's.

When she answered the door, she looked in a state. "I don't know what to do. They're *really* sick. Should I call the doctor? Or take them to the hospital?"

I was confident that my tonic would do the trick, so I suggested she give them each a dose and if there was no improvement in a couple of hours, then she could think about doctors and hospitals.

She looked dubious. "You're sure this will work?"

"It's a home remedy perfected by my grandmother." I reminded her. And hers before that...

KATHLEEN PICKED me up in her grocery van and we headed off. Ballydehag was a small enough village that we didn't have to go far before we were in the Irish countryside, where sheep and cows grazed in the green fields and where we would soon forage in woodlands. We didn't have a long way to drive, maybe twenty minutes, during which time I told her about the sick American guests.

"Whisht, why ever didn't you tell me before? I've a tonic that will set them right up."

"Because I made one of my own that I delivered this morning." I tried not to sound irked, but really.

She drove on. "If it doesn't work, I'll drop by with mine."

I rolled my eyes but kept my mouth shut. If we weren't careful, Kathleen and I would end up like Oscar Wilde and Bartholomew Branson.

She pulled up at the side of a road where there was a lay-by.

"Now don't tell everybody about this spot," she told me. "It's a privilege that I'm even bringing you here."

I completely understood what she meant. We all have our special places where we like to pick certain herbs and berries and so on. I answered quite seriously that I was honored, and I wouldn't tell another soul.

Then she relented. "It was Lucinda who first introduced me to the area, anyway."

Lucinda was the witch who had had The Blarney Tome before me. She'd been banished to England somewhere for some crime, and nobody had ever told me what that was. I had, in turn, been banished here for trying to cheat death. Not for me, which probably would have been even worse, but for my ex-husband. Anyway, I was here now and happy to be following quite literally in Lucinda's footsteps. Since I lived in her house and ran her shop, I'd come to feel a kinship for my sister witch. We secretly communicated through a scrying mirror, usually when I needed advice about the shop. We were careful not to do it very often as if we got found out, we'd get in even more trouble than we already were.

Kathleen and I plunged into the woods along a barely discernible path. We didn't get far before she was pointing out berries for making sloe gin. They looked like large, dark blueberries.

"We'll come back after the first frost," she said. "That's when you harvest the berries from the Blackthorn tree."

We found gorgeous fat red rosehips, several mushroom varieties that were new to me, and then she showed me a low bush. "Oh," I said, "funny to find bay leaves out here. Do they grow wild in Ireland?"

She gave me a superior smirk. "That's an easy mistake to make, Quinn. But these are Cherry Laurel and quite deadly. I have a recipe for making an ointment from the Cherry Laurel that's a cure for ringworm, but there's not much call for that these days."

We moved on to a fine patch of nettles.

Kathleen crouched before a cluster of the green-leaved plants, and I found my own. We didn't take too much. Nature is bounteous, but we're always careful not to deplete her resources. I placed my gathered herbs into one of the small bags I'd brought especially for the purpose and tucked it into the foraging bag. As I was about to rise, I noticed something glinting. I picked it up.

"This is odd," I said. The object in my hand was a brass button, quite ornate. I'd have said it was old, but it was shiny and clean enough that it obviously hadn't been outside for long.

"What's that you've got there?" Kathleen asked me.

I held up my palm to better show her.

"Unusual place to find an untarnished brass button."

"I know," I said, puzzled. "It doesn't look like it's been here long. Somebody else must know about your secret spot." I shielded my eyes as I scanned the area.

Nothing came in view but a small stone cottage that had seen better days. The thatched roof was in good repair, otherwise the little house appeared abandoned. If I hadn't been searching for the owner of a lost button, I wouldn't even have noticed the cottage.

"That looks lonely," I said to Kathleen.

She rose to stand. "I think that's the point. Glyn McTavish lives there. They say he was a Dubliner who went to America as a young man. Nobody knows what happened there, but we suspect a heartbreak because when he came back to Ireland, he moved into this cottage and became a complete recluse. What you might call a hermit."

"He must be. I've not only never seen him, but I've never even heard of him."

"You wouldn't have. He gets most everything delivered."

"Not a great reader, then," I couldn't help commenting. If I was stuck in a little cottage all by myself, I'd at least read a lot of books. For all I knew, he had an e-reader, but it seemed odd to think of something so modern in a cottage so old. Was there even power and internet out here?

"I believe he does like a good book, but perhaps he gets them elsewhere."

"I'm not fond of people who don't support local businesses," I said. I should definitely get to know this Glyn McTavish. If he got everything delivered, and he liked to read, I'd be more than happy to deliver books to him, and do a little foraging while I was out this way.

"He probably doesn't know The Blarney Tome even exists," she said in a soothing tone.

"I guess he won't invite us in for coffee," I said. I'd finished my thermos long ago and could dearly use another cup.

"You must be joking. He won't even see me, and I'm the person standing between him and starvation. When I deliver his box of food, I knock on his door and leave his groceries in front of it." She shook her head and her gray curls bobbed. "The only way I know he's still alive is because of the smoke coming out of his chimney."

I stared at the cottage. The chimney had no smoke, and it was a cool fall day. Not too cold if you were foraging while wrapped up warm in outdoor clothing. But to be inside a stone cottage with a thatched roof? If it was me, I'd have the fire going for sure.

Not so much as a puff of smoke came from the old chimney. Kathleen and I turned to each other.

"Perhaps we should make sure he's simply let the fire die," she said.

I agreed, but I felt a shiver along my arms as we headed toward that lonely little house. Perhaps Glyn McTavish was also a forager and was tramping in the woods. Or he could have taken an unexpected trip elsewhere. I tried to believe these things, but with every step closer to the cottage, my senses picked up on something dark.

"Oh, dear," Kathleen said, and I knew she was sensing it too. She strode quickly toward the cottage now. "Perhaps he's sick. For all we know, the poor man's fallen, broken a leg, and is shivering on the floor."

I hoped she was right, I really did. But what I sensed inside that cottage was darker than a broken leg.

CHAPTER 5

Weeds and long grasses tangled around my jean-clad legs as we walked swiftly toward Glyn McTavish's thatched cottage. It was so lonely sitting in the middle of this field and the lack of smoke coming out of the chimney made it seem bereft somehow. The weather didn't help. I imagined in the spring and summer when the flowers were blooming, this would be pretty enough. But today was one of those damp Irish days that could chill you to the bone.

It wasn't only the damp chilling me to the bone. Every instinct in my body told me to turn and run. The darkness I felt coming from that small stone cottage was not welcoming.

I wondered what it was doing here all by itself. Perhaps once it had been a shepherd's hut, but there were no sheep anywhere near or any other activity to suggest another trade. As though it were built for a hermit or an outcast.

When we climbed two steps to a small porch, I saw a chair beside the door. It was solid wood and more utilitarian than beautiful. I heard a woodpecker in the vicinity, but otherwise the silence was perfect. We paused at the sturdy front door to glance at each other. Then, taking a deep breath, Kathleen raised her hand and knocked.

No one answered.

She knocked a second time and still nothing. The woodpecker had stopped now so the sound of her knuckles thudding on the door seemed to echo.

After another minute of silence, Kathleen called through the door, "Glyn McTavish? It's Kathleen McGinnis from Finnegan's Grocery. Just wanting to check that you're all right."

More silence.

I said, "Well, if he's not answering, then there's nothing we can do."

"We can peek in the windows."

I stared at her. "Who's to say he doesn't have a shotgun in there? Is he the kind of recluse who might shoot first and ask questions later?"

She shook her head. "Quinn, when will you accept you're in Ireland and not the United States of America?"

I knew she was right. That there were a lot fewer guns here, but farmers still owned shotguns. I bet isolated hermits owned them as well.

Still, when she went one way to peek in the windows, I went the other way. There were shutters on all the windows and each was shut tight.

"He doesn't like light, does he?" I called out to Kathleen.

"He's a strange individual. Still, I can't help but think there's something wrong."

I was feeling the same thing. When we met back at the

front door, Kathleen knocked again. "I could use a spell to open it, but he would not be best pleased if he's avoiding us."

I'd thought the same.

We stood there another few seconds, then, almost as an afterthought, she tried the door. The handle turned. It wasn't locked.

Why would a man go to such lengths to shut out all the light by closing and shuttering all the windows but leave his door unlocked? It didn't make sense. The eerie feeling I had grew stronger.

Kathleen hesitated. We both did. And then she pushed the door wide open.

It was dim inside, of course, with all the windows shuttered. We left the door open behind us, perhaps so we could run if we needed to. On such a cloudy day, there wasn't much light from the doorway, so it took us a minute to become accustomed to the gloom.

I was aware first of the smell of smoke. The fire wasn't burning now, but it hadn't been that long since it had gone out. I felt odd walking into this stranger's home, especially knowing that he didn't encourage visitors, but we were on a charity mission, after all. I went to the closest window and opened the shutters. At the other end of the small home, Kathleen did the same. Then she reached for a light switch and to my amazement, an overhead light went on. This cottage couldn't be connected to the city's electricity. It had to be off-grid. No doubt Glyn McTavish had a generator.

Inside, the home had a comfort and coziness that wasn't apparent on the outside. We were in a great room with beamed ceilings, kitchen cupboards painted blue, a flagstone floor, a big fireplace where I could still smell the smoke of a recent fire, and also a woodstove.

The furniture was sturdy and appeared relatively new. Books lined one wall and a comfortable chair sat by the fireplace. This was the kind of place that could be fun for a week or so, but to live here full-time? I couldn't imagine not going mad with loneliness.

The hermit was a tidy man. Apart from an empty cardboard box beside the bookcase, everything had been put away. I noticed the number 4 written on the box in pen. No doubt Kathleen numbered her deliveries. Made sense.

I could imagine it would be pretty cozy sitting by the fire with a good book and a cup of tea. But surely it would be lonely.

There were two closed doors. Kathleen opened one to reveal a bathroom. The other door must lead to the bedroom.

Kathleen nibbled her lower lip as if unsure what to do, then she knocked on the second door.

There was no answer.

She called out softly, "Glyn? Are you in there?"

Nothing. She rapped louder this time and repeated her question.

Still nothing.

When she opened the door, I came up behind her and looked over her shoulder and into the room.

Neither of us said a word. I found a switch just inside the door, and the room sprang to light.

I really wished I hadn't turned on the light. We could see him there. On the floor, face down. He was long and thin with wispy gray hair. Wearing pajamas. His feet were bare, which made him seem so vulnerable in the cold. I felt a bizarre urge to cover him with a blanket though I suspected he was beyond feeling the cold.

I went forward, dropped to my knees, and placed my fingers on his throat where I'd expect to find a pulse. Even before I touched his skin, I knew there wouldn't be one. He was already cold. Almost as cold as the stone floor he lay on.

"What do you think happened to him?" Kathleen asked. "Could he have fallen out of bed and hit his head?"

I stood up slowly and scanned the room. "Oh no," I said when I saw the bowl on his bedside table.

Kathleen followed my gaze. "It can't be," she said, her voice reedy with shock.

We could see what he'd eaten before going to bed. The bowl was all but finished, but there were still a few chunks of Irish stew in the bottom.

We shared a horrified glance.

"Poor Sean," was all Kathleen said.

I knew exactly what she meant. Without meaning to, it seemed like the owner of our favorite pub had accidentally killed one of his customers.

I backed away, leaving the poor dead man on the floor. "We have to call the police."

"Aye, the Gardaí must be notified," she said, sounding sad.

"We don't know for sure that he was killed by the Irish stew," I said. "Or that it was Sean's. More than likely a recluse cooked his own food." Even as I said it, I recalled how clean the kitchen had been. There was no sign of recently washed pots; no scent of cooking remained in the air.

Kathleen shook her head. "Sean O'Grady often delivered meals to Glyn."

Well, that was one customer he wouldn't be serving again.

I was very much afraid that it would be a long time before Sean would be serving food to anyone.

"This is a bad, sad day, Quinn," Kathleen said, pulling out her cell phone.

"Yes. It is." I settled down with my bag of foraged herbs to wait for the police.

CHAPTER 6

I sat quietly, wishing Glyn's departing spirit godspeed. It was difficult to concentrate, though, because once Kathleen had called emergency services, she could not settle. It might have been that there was only one chair. I offered it to her, but she shook her head and kept pacing and muttering to herself. Not spells either, those I'd have recognized. Hers were the mutterings of a disturbed mind. And in such a small space, she only managed three strides before she had to turn around again.

Finally, she said very clearly, "He must have hit his head. I'm sure that's what happened, Quinn. Imagine this. Glyn McTavish got out of bed in the night for the loo. He was a little disoriented. With no light on, he tangled his foot in the bedclothes and tumbled. Poor man. He must have hit his head on the flagstone floor." She stomped her booted foot vigorously as though to prove her point. Not that there was any doubt the floor was made of stone. I certainly wasn't arguing with her on that point.

When I didn't comment, she went back to her pacing.

Then she stopped suddenly and turned to me again. "Or it could have been a heart attack. A man like that, living all alone. I bet he hadn't seen the inside of a surgery in some long time."

I was about to ask why the hermit had needed surgery and then realized of course that she meant surgery in the Irish term, as in a doctor's office. "Are you saying he was ill?"

She looked irritated as though I'd said something really stupid. "How can I tell if he was ill? How could anyone? As far as I know, he never went outside the walls of this house. Any number of things could kill an eejit who had no medical care. He could have easily had a heart attack or a stroke."

"Were you friendly with the hermit?" I had to ask because I'd never seen Kathleen this agitated before.

Her energy jangled around the room like out-of-tune bells. It was very disconcerting.

She threw up her hands. "How could you know a man who only had one chair? And none to offer a visitor?" She pointed to the single chair I was sitting on as though I might not have noticed that this wasn't exactly a home that welcomed guests.

And then it hit me. Slower than it should have because I'd been focusing on the dead man. Last night, she'd slipped in to visit 'little Bridget,' who had been working in Sean's pub's kitchen. That's what was making her so agitated. "You're worried about your cousin's daughter. Did she make the stew?"

"Little Bridget was stirring the stew pot when I went into the kitchen to visit. So proud she was that Sean O'Grady was giving her proper food-preparing tasks to do, and not just the washing-up, which she'd expected."

Another thought occurred to me. Had Kathleen interfered when she'd visited to make sure the girl was doing okay?

I rose from Glyn McTavish's chair like an avenging angel. "Kathleen, did you put something in Sean's stew?"

For the first time she changed her course. Instead of crossing the cottage wall to wall, she turned her back to me and paced toward the small kitchen.

I took a step toward her. "Kathleen!" I said her name quite firmly this time.

When she finally faced me, her eyes were full of tears, her face a mask of misery. "I only wanted to help. I could see she was nervous, poor wee Bridget. Terribly worried she wouldn't please Sean O'Grady. It was the work of a moment. I only whispered a few words over the bubbling stew." But her gaze had dropped to the floor. I did not believe her.

"Kathleen..."

She clasped her hands so tight the skin went white and I could see lines of dirt where she'd harvested the more delicate herbs without wearing her gloves. "Fine! If you must know, and I'll have no peace until you stop badgering me, I thought the stew a tad bland. I added a little more spice."

I felt the blood drain from my face. "What, exactly, did you add?"

She looked furious with me, but in a guilty way. "I'll thank you to know, I'm a fine cook, and I have been a practicing witch since before you were born, young lady."

I let go of the argument that she'd been practicing that long. If she wanted to think I was younger than I was, I wasn't going to take issue. Besides, that wasn't the point. I couldn't help but notice she hadn't answered the question.

"The police are going to be here soon. One of us is going to have to tell them that you added something to that stew."

She went paler than my face felt, paler than the flagstone floor. Honestly, some of my book club vampires had more color in their cheeks. Afraid she might faint, I took a step closer to her.

"Surely that's not necessary?" She banged her fist on the scrubbed pine table. "We live peaceably here, you and I and those of our kind. Stop, Quinn, and think for a moment. If you speak up and say a witch put something into a stew that's killed people or even just made them ill, can you imagine the repercussions?"

A shudder went over my flesh. Instinctively. It's carried in the DNA of all witches, our sad, tragic, and painful history. Sure, some of the witches like Biddy O'Donnell probably deserved to be hanged, but most of the women who'd been murdered had been healers. Kathleen and I were healers. Maybe we occasionally interfered in people's business where we didn't necessarily belong, but we meant well. Whatever she had done, she had meant well. Still, we had to do what was right.

I said, more gently now, "You cannot let Bridget take the fall for this."

She dashed a tear from her cheek. "Don't you think I know that? I'm wracking my brain to think how else this terrible thing might have happened."

I didn't blame her. I was wracking my own brain so hard I was getting a headache. Trouble was, there was a nearly empty bowl of Irish stew sitting beside the dead man's bed. And we already knew that very same stew had made two hale and hearty young New Yorkers violently ill. Putting that two and two together was not complicated math.

"Is Bridget..." I hesitated to find the right words. "One of us?" With the dead man lying in the next room, I hesitated to use the word witch.

Her face lightened in a sudden smile. "Bridget's no more magic in her than that table there." She looked at it consideringly. "Less, probably."

While she paced, I went toward the shelves of books. It was something to do while we waited for the Gardaí to arrive. I couldn't help myself, if there were books in a room, I had to check them out. An occupational hazard now I ran a bookshop, though I was always a snooper of bookshelves. What people displayed on those shelves said so much about them. Did Glyn McTavish prefer literary fiction? Detective novels? Science Fiction? Non-fiction? I scanned the shelves and saw all of the above. In such an orderly house, I was surprised at how random the arrangement was. As a bookseller, I was accustomed to placing volumes like with like, so all the thrillers would sit together. Then within that system, I kept the books alphabetically ordered so, for example, Bartholomew Branson was ahead of Dan Brown, which always pleased Bartholomew.

Glyn McTavish, however, had no system I could detect. Literary fiction sat beside a book on composting, nudging a volume of Wordsworth's poetry, beside what I suspected based on its binding was a first edition of James Joyce's Ulysses. I'd have checked, but I didn't want to put my fingerprints on anything inside this cottage of death.

We both jumped when there was a rap on the door. We looked at each other. Kathleen said, in a low, begging voice,

"Please, Quinn. Don't say anything quite yet. Give me some time."

Equally softly, I said, "There isn't going to be much time."

I felt for her, I really did. I knew she'd only been trying to help her cousin's daughter do better in her job, but the truth was she'd interfered where she had no business and with tragic results. Still, she was a sister. She'd been good to me. And I knew Kathleen wouldn't let Bridget suffer for a mistake she'd made. I nodded and then went to open the door.

Two uniformed Gardaí stood outside. Coming up the path behind them were Detective Inspector Walsh and his sidekick Sergeant Kelly.

I'd never seen the two Gardaí officers before, but unfortunately, the pair of Gardaí detectives were familiar to me. On seeing me standing in the doorway, Sergeant Kelly raised an eyebrow as though to say, You again?

I was really going to have to stop showing up at murder scenes. It wasn't good for my reputation.

The two detectives donned those paper boot things and surgical gloves and went into Glyn's bedroom. I could hear them moving around and their low murmuring. Then the chink of china on wood as though one of them had picked up the bowl of stew and sniffed it and put it back. Kathleen and I shared a frightened glance.

The two Gardaí officers remained by the door, not seeming to know what else to do with themselves. We clearly weren't a flight risk, but obviously they couldn't let us go or let anyone else in, unless it was the authorities. Not that poor Glyn McTavish had been in the habit of entertaining streams of visitors.

After a couple of uncomfortable minutes, Detective

Inspector Walsh came out, leaving Sergeant Kelly still in the room with the dead man. No doubt the sergeant was going through the room or whatever sordid tasks he had to do when someone died suddenly.

Before DI Walsh could open his mouth, Kathleen jumped in. Oh, that jangling energy was even worse now. It was like fingernails on a blackboard screeching all around me.

"Did he have a heart attack?" she asked too quickly.

The detective inspector turned to her, his gaze very steady on her face. "Why would you think that?"

She shrugged and gave some version of the argument she'd made to me. McTavish was an older man and a recluse. He hadn't been in the habit of going to the doctor.

"So, you knew the gentleman, then?" DI Walsh asked her.

That's what she got for jumping into speech so quickly. I should have told her to keep her mouth shut and wait for them to ask questions. Kathleen wasn't thinking clearly right now. That much was obvious.

She glanced around the tiny cottage and back at the inspector. "Not really. That is to say, I didn't know the man well, but I delivered groceries to him. He didn't appear to go out much."

The detective inspector studied McTavish's space without looking very surprised. Then he focused on me.

"Did either of you touch the body?"

Why is it that they always do that? Immediately make a person feel like they've interfered with an important murder investigation when all you were trying to do was check vital signs? To get help if the person needed it. I put my chin up.

"I did. I wanted to make sure...if he was still alive...I thought he might need an ambulance."

"And did you move him at all?"

"No!" The very idea was horrifying. "All I did was this." I put my two fingers together and demonstrated checking the jugular vein in my own throat. No question I was alive. My pulse was jumping like a chihuahua spying a dog treat.

DI Walsh nodded. And still, in that conversational tone, asked, "And did you touch anything else in the room?"

We both shook our heads.

"He was already cold," I said, just in case the detective inspector might have wondered. I imagined in this wintry atmosphere and lying on that stone floor, McTavish had cooled off very quickly.

DI Walsh nodded again. Then, as though we were just having a pleasant conversation, he asked, "And what were you two doing visiting the gentleman?" He didn't bother to say that it was pretty clear the hermit didn't get a lot of visitors.

Before Kathleen could put her foot in it again, I said simply, "We were foraging in the area." I pointed to my bag of herbs. I hoped very much he had no witch lore because some of my gatherings were definitely not used in cooking.

"Why did you enter his house?" DI Walsh asked.

Again, I went with the truth. "We noticed there was no smoke coming from his chimney and wanted to make sure he was all right." Now that I put it into words, our actions seemed officious rather than charitable. Or was I viewing every action the way the detective inspector might?

He studied my foraging bag without touching it. Kathleen's was on the floor beside it. Ages seemed to go by. No one said anything. I felt like we were all listening to the sergeant inside the bedroom. I could hear his voice as though he was talking to someone. I wondered if he was recording the scene and his findings. Modern smartphones must make policing a whole lot easier.

At the end of an eternity, the sergeant came out. He glanced at the inspector and said, "Can I speak to you outside for a minute, sir?"

My heart sank. I felt as guilty as if I had killed the poor hermit. The two detectives went outside and, weirdly, the two Gardaí officers now stiffened to attention and made sure they blocked the path between us and the door. They'd come to the conclusion that Kathleen and I were dangerous in some way. Oh, great.

It was only about five minutes until the detectives returned, but it felt like as many years.

DI Walsh looked at Kathleen and then me and said, "You can go now. But we may need to speak to you again."

"Of course," Kathleen and I both said at once.

I headed toward the door, and it seemed almost with reluctance that the two Gardaí officers parted for me.

When I reached for my foraging bag, the detective inspector said, "Leave that there, please."

I glanced back at him, startled, but just nodded. Kathleen, however, was still too rattled to be wise.

She said, "Whatever do you want those for? It's just some herbs and things. We make soaps and use them in cooking." Her voice had risen more than she probably realized on the word cooking.

He merely said, "You'll get them back when we've finished with them."

I took her arm before she could say another word. Together we walked out the front door of the cottage. I think both of us pretty much wished we'd never entered it in the first place.

As we staggered toward the car, Kathleen said, "I'm with you, Quinn. It's time to get a nice, hot cup of coffee."

I laughed, a sort of hysterical sound. "I am way past coffee. This is a time for something stronger."

Besides, I really needed to see what was going on at the pub and restaurant.

CHAPTER 7

Given Kathleen's emotional state, I was a little worried about her driving, so I kept a vigilant eye out for other traffic, woodland animals that might scamper across our path, or any hazard, really. That's how I came to see such a curious sight. I caught a glimpse of what I was certain was a feather, but it wasn't attached to a bird flying. I watched as the feather bobbed again from behind some bushes. The third time I recognized it as part of a hat. Sort of an old-fashioned hat with a high brim and a feather on it. I wondered for a moment if it was a child playing dress-up as the person underneath the hat wasn't very tall.

I must have made a sound even though I didn't know I had because Kathleen turned and said, "What is it?"

She didn't sound too upset and her driving had been perfectly fine so far, so I said, "There's an old-fashioned hat bobbing around in the woods. I guess it must be a child playing dress-up or something." Though even as I said it, I thought it was a strange place to play dress-up. And how many kids lived around here?

She slanted me a funny look.

"What?" I asked sharply. I'd had enough surprises for one day.

She shook her head as though disappointed in me. "Really, Quinn. Have you not been in Ireland this long without coming across a leprechaun?"

Honestly, my eyes nearly bugged out of my head. I'm a witch, so I get that there are creatures that are, let's just say, outside of the mainstream. I ran a book club for vampires, for goodness sake. But in all my forty-five years I had never, ever heard tell that leprechauns were real. Even now, after our harrowing morning, I wasn't entirely sure she wasn't making fun of me. Let's see what the gullible American will swallow this time. Yes, I'd had a few locals play that game with me. But Kathleen didn't appear to be in a joking mood.

"Leprechauns? Are you kidding me?" At least I could put on a skeptical attitude, then if she was messing with me, I wouldn't look quite so naïve.

But she didn't even crack the faintest of smiles. "Of course, leprechauns. I won't say it's every day you'll be seeing them. But believe me, they're never far away."

All I could think of was drunken fools dressed up on St. Patrick's Day. The mythology I knew about leprechauns would pretty much fit inside a green beer mug.

"Leprechauns. They're small in stature, bring you good luck, and at the end of the rainbow there's a pot of gold." I thought for a minute. "Oh, and aren't they generally cobblers?"

Something flashed across my mind. Cobbler was such an old-fashioned term, but I had heard the word recently. Where?

Kathleen was mainly keeping her gaze on the road, but I could tell she was also watching me out of the corner of her eye. And then it hit me. "The new family who took over the bakery."

She didn't say anything but her lips tilted up in a tiny smile. Was I on the right track or was she really having fun with me?

"I went to introduce myself. He called me mistress and said something about learning a new trade. I recall the conversation definitely had the word cobbler in there. You're saying Paddy McGrath is a leprechaun? Oh, and he mentioned a wife."

"If we've a family of leprechauns who've moved into Ballydehag, the question is, why?"

I shrugged. "Don't they need jobs like everybody else? Baking and selling bread is a perfectly respected profession. I can't imagine there'd be enough people needing their shoes fixed in Ballydehag for them to make a living at shoe repair."

"Quinn, don't believe everything you've read in the fairy tales. Leprechauns are a nasty, low, thieving, butcherous set of little people."

I had to make allowances for the fact that every magical creature seemed to have it in for some other magical creature, but she really sounded quite angry with the poor leprechauns.

"What did they ever do to you?"

She said, "It's more a question of what they'll do to you if you get in the way of their foul schemes."

I finally became too stunned to speak. Not only had leprechauns turned out to be real, but they weren't sweet little creatures dancing jigs and finding pots of gold at the end of rainbows? Some childish spark in me was extinguished in that moment. I lived with magic. And I always wanted to believe in the best of it, even as I commonly came across the darker aspects. But leprechauns? It was like finding out my teddy bear was secretly plotting against me. Sad and very unsettling.

"What do you think they're doing in Ballydehag?"

"I don't know, Quinn, but I'll tell you something for nothing, they're not here to bake bread."

"Maybe they are. Maybe we should give them a chance. Don't you think you're being a bit judgmental?"

Even though the bakery would technically be competition for Kathleen's grocery, I didn't think she'd mind any more than the rest of us did if we finally got some decent, fresh bread in town. So I didn't think it was professional jealousy causing her negative attitude. Something must have happened.

"Come on, we've still got twenty minutes until we get back to town. You must have had a bad experience. Why don't you tell me about it? It'll help pass the time."

She shook her head and merely said, "Don't you take this lightly, Quinn. Leprechauns are not a joking matter."

And more she would not say.

We were both silent for a little while and then suddenly she said, "What do you think the detectives want with our herbs?"

I shook my head. I'd been trying not to think about them confiscating our foraging bags. "Probably they're just being thorough."

"They can't possibly know about people getting sick from Sean's Irish stew last night."

"You don't know that." I had a terrible thought. Maybe one of those Americans had died. I didn't say anything to Kathleen as she was stressed enough, and I didn't want to add our deaths to whatever today's tally might be by making her drive off the road. However, if there'd been a second fatality around Irish stew, well, if I was a detective and found two women with bags of herbs in a little stone cottage where a dead guy was lying beside a half-eaten bowl of stew, I guess I'd be confiscating their herbs too. A shudder went over me. When was I going to stop getting myself into trouble?

Not, in fairness, that this was my doing. Kathleen was the one who wanted to go foraging, and Kathleen was the one who knew Glyn McTavish. Still, we had mutually decided to go check on his welfare when we'd both noticed that no smoke was coming out of his chimney, and I so wished we hadn't.

She rolled the grocery van right past her store, and then mine, and headed for the pub. The small parking lot was empty but for two cars, but there were lights on inside. I hesitated before I opened my door.

"Are you sure we should go in? If the police find us there..."

"We must go in. I must check on poor little Bridget. And we must talk to Sean. If anyone has any idea what happened last night, it will be him."

She was right, of course, and I was as anxious as she was to get to the bottom of this mystery. Okay, maybe slightly less anxious than she was, since I hadn't put anything in a potentially deadly stew and my relative wasn't likely to get blamed for it, but I still felt a keen interest in the case.

THE PUB DOOR wasn't locked so Kathleen and I walked in. The usually convivial space could not have been more different than the night before. No music was playing. No sound of laughter and no chinking of glasses. No thud of darts on the dartboard. It was as somber as a tomb. And even as that word floated through my consciousness, I shuddered. I wondered if dining on pub food might have contributed to at least one person ending up in their tomb.

We both stood, uncertain, not quite knowing what to do. I took a step deeper and noticed that Sean wasn't behind the bar as he usually was. He was sitting on a stool slumped over the bar like the most miserable of customers. It was a shocking image.

He was only in his thirties, young and attractive in that distinctly Irish way, with his wavy black hair and piercing blue eyes. He usually had a joke and a flirty word for all the women, no matter how old and staid we might be. He was probably one of the most popular people in the town. To see him sitting there, his hair disheveled from where he'd been gripping it with his fingers, his face wan, and his posture dejected, was awful. When he turned to look at us, I could see his eyes were bloodshot.

"I'm not really open," he said, but so halfheartedly I wanted to throw my arms around him.

"We heard." I went right up and sat beside him, in case he wanted to talk. "What happened?"

"I've no idea. In all my years running pubs and all the restaurants I've worked in, I've never had a bad review. And for people to say they're deathly ill, and blame it on the pub, without even talking to me first, isn't right. And not only that, they weren't too sick to put the same review on every public forum they could find." He took another swig of his drink. "And they didn't even use real names so I could ring them up. Called themselves BadluckoftheIrish. Who would do such a thing?"

I glanced at Kathleen. I hadn't heard that. As gently as I could, and knowing that a certain detective would have my head for what I was about to do, I asked, "Sean, did you deliver any of your stew last night?"

He drank deeply of his whiskey. I could tell this wasn't his first. He pushed the bottle toward us and told Kathleen to get a couple more glasses down from the bar. She did. He clearly didn't want to be alone in his misery.

"What's that got to do with anything?" he asked. He wasn't slurring yet, but I didn't think he was too far off. "I do a bit of delivery, sure. Have to around these parts. There aren't enough customers to keep us going otherwise."

"Who did the deliveries last night?"

He squinted at me. "Is there a purpose to this questioning, Quinn? Because otherwise, I've a bottle to get through."

Kathleen sat on the stool next to me so Sean didn't have to swivel to look at both of us. He poured us both very healthy glasses of Irish whiskey. Honestly, it's an acquired taste, and one I hadn't acquired yet, but I didn't want to break the mood by asking for white wine instead. Besides, there are times in one's life when Irish whiskey seems like the answer. Like after you stumble on a dead body, for instance. I took a sip and tried not to grimace. I felt like I might have to take up fire-eating as a sport to condition myself for this drink.

I didn't say anything and Kathleen was smart enough not to say anything either, so my question floated in the air.

Finally, Sean said, "We were short-staffed last night. Bridget can't drive, so I left her stirring the stew and did the deliveries myself."

My heart began to thump a little faster. "Do you remember who you delivered to?"

He looked like he was going to get lippy with me again, but Kathleen said gently, "It's important, Sean."

He might not have known me all that long, but he'd known Kathleen for years and obviously trusted her. He nodded briefly. "Should I get my order book?"

"Which ones do you remember?" she asked.

He stared into his whiskey as though the names might be written there. "I did a circuit to be efficient with time and petrol. Let's see, first stop was the Bailey family. Two sausage and mash and an extra helping of chips."

He listed off a few more names, but I only took note of those who had ordered Irish stew. There were two. The O'Tooles and the Kennedy family. I suspected one of them might be known online as BadluckoftheIrish. Then, finally, he'd driven to Glyn McTavish's cottage and delivered his stew. I felt my heart sink into my boots. Even though we'd known it was the most likely explanation for that stew sitting beside Glyn's bed, I'd still hoped desperately there would be another explanation.

"Did you talk to Glyn McTavish?" I asked.

"Never do. He has the stew every Friday. As usual, I set the bag on his front porch, banged on the door, and left. I'm a busy man. I don't have time to chat when I'm doing deliveries, especially not to a man who doesn't care to open his door when you knock on it. The pub was busy and I was short-handed so I drove back to O'Brien's as fast as I could."

"And it was just one order of the stew? He didn't order anything else?"

Sean uttered a laugh that sounded more like a snort. "What? You think he had a lady friend? If I ever was asked to take more than one dish to Glyn McTavish, I'd have put a bulletin in the newspaper."

I knew I was really getting in the police's business here but I had to know, and surely Kathleen wanted the same information. "You said you only left Bridget stirring the stew. Did you make it?"

He sat up straighter and looked quite offended. "Naturally, I made the stew. You think I'd leave some green kitchen helper with one of the dishes I'm famous for? Not ruddy likely."

I felt abashed and apologized. And really felt like kicking Kathleen's ankle. Last night, she'd interfered with Sean O'Grady's stew for nothing.

"It was the same as I always make," he went on. "I don't deviate from the recipe. Got the lamb good and fresh from Sean Higgins, as I always do."

Sean Higgins was the local butcher. He might have shared a first name with Sean O'Grady, but the two men couldn't have been more different. Sean Higgins was a terrifying man with huge tattooed arms who had no love for me. Nor had his wife, Rosie, who helped him in the shop. There'd been a time when I thought they'd up and leave Ballydehag, because the whole town knew she'd been unfaithful. Still, they'd stayed and the two of them seemed to muddle along.

Was it possible that the source of the problem was the

butcher? Could his lamb have been bad? When Kathleen nudged me, I knew she was thinking the same.

"Vegetables are all local. I have them delivered every week." He shook his head. "I've gone over and over it and can't work out how it could have happened."

If he was this upset now, he was going to be apoplectic when the police paid him a visit, which they'd probably do soon.

What would he do when he discovered his Irish stew hadn't just made people sick, but had killed someone?

CHAPTER 8

Kathleen dropped me back at my cottage and naturally I told Cerridwen about the distressing adventures of the morning. I made myself a cup of coffee, partly to get the taste of harsh whiskey out of my mouth and partly to warm up. I felt chilled to the bone, not just from cold.

Death is a chilling business. Unlike Kathleen, I didn't think for a minute that Glyn McTavish had had a heart attack or tripped himself up in the bedclothes and fallen to his death. By accident or design, there was another hand involved. I was certain of it.

When I sat down with my coffee, Cerridwen jumped up in my lap. I was so grateful. I needed both her warmth and her comfort. And her listening ear. Unfortunately, she's no Puss in Boots and isn't inclined to talk back. After a while, I felt like I needed an impartial pair of ears to listen to this tangled tale. And really, someone I genuinely trusted who knew the truth about leprechauns. Deep down I still wasn't certain that Kathleen hadn't been messing with me.

If they were real and as nasty as Kathleen seemed to think, then what did it mean that I'd seen one near McTavish's cottage this morning?

There was only one person I could think of to talk to. Lochlan Balfour. I wouldn't say he was humorless because he had a certain sly humor uniquely his own, but I knew he would never joke about something like the existence of leprechauns. Also, he'd been around so long and seen so much that there wasn't much he didn't know. And he was an excellent listener.

He also didn't seem to need much sleep. I glanced at the clock and thought there was a very good chance he was still awake.

I called his cell phone, and he picked up right away. After I'd asked if he was busy, he immediately said, "Quinn, what's wrong?"

Sensitive too, which is a nice thing to have in a friend. And a vampire.

"There's something I want to talk to you about. Do you have a minute?"

His chuckle was low. "I have all the time in the world." There was a hint of self-mockery because, of course, he did. "Do you want me to come over?"

Did I? Did I want the tall, gorgeous vampire in my small space? What if the police came? I said, "No. I'll come to you."

"I'll get the coffee on."

His words made me smile. He knew me too well.

Before I could hang up, he said, "And shall I get Dierdre to run your bookshop for the rest of the day?"

It was like he could read my mind. "Not for the whole day, but maybe for a couple more hours. If she doesn't mind."

He chuckled again. "I have more trouble keeping Dierdre out of The Blarney Tome than you can imagine. She needs a hobby."

One thing at a time.

The day was warming, crisp and green, as I rode my bicycle the short distance to Devil's Keep. When I got there, Lochlan opened the door himself. He stared at my face.

"Quinn, you look troubled."

I just nodded.

"Come in."

You would never know from the gloomy and very historic-looking exterior how high-tech the interior of Lochlan's castle was. I admired the way he'd kept the old stone and the architectural features of the various ages, the medieval drawbridge, the gothic windows, and so on, but he'd also made a very livable, modern space. Almost no natural light penetrated the castle. In ancient times, I think it was to keep the heat of the fires inside and probably to give the castle's enemies fewer spaces through which to launch their arrows. But, for your modern vampire, it offered excellent protection from the sunlight.

There were lots of bedrooms, and turrets, and dungeons offering plenty of space for the extra undead guests who seemed to come and go or live permanently with Lochlan. They were a motley crew, but he kept them in check pretty well. Mostly, I think, he made sure they were busy. The late-night vampire book club we ran in my shop was just one of the many activities he'd organized to keep the bored creatures out of trouble.

Not that it always worked. Some of his recent houseguests were more than usually troublesome.

He led me upstairs to his private apartments. Even though he didn't drink coffee, he owned an espresso machine that any barista would drool over. He didn't ask me what I wanted because he knew. In less than a minute, a perfect cappuccino was at my elbow, along with a couple of almond biscotti.

I took a fortifying sip and then I began to talk, spilling out the whole sorry tale, starting with last night to the events of the morning. He listened to all of it and then his first comment was a curious one.

He said, "Leprechauns. Hmm."

I waited for what Lochlan would say next. He stared over my shoulder as though there were something interesting in the far corner of the room. I knew he'd speak up when he had something to say, so I kept my impatience to myself. Finally, he brought his gaze back to my face.

"And you're sure they're leprechauns who have taken over the bakery?"

I said, "I'm not sure of anything."

"And Glyn McTavish is dead."

"Okay, that I'm sure of. And I think I saw a leprechaun near his cottage when Kathleen and I drove away this morning." I hated to ask my next question. I mean, I'd eaten Lucky Charms, and I'd seen Darby O'Gill and the Little People. "Could the leprechauns have killed Glyn McTavish?" Even as I said it, I felt terrible. It was like accusing the Easter Bunny of being an ax murderer.

However, Lochlan didn't seem to think my question was crazy as it sounded in my ears. He considered the matter carefully. "I've never known them to be murderous. Greed is their besetting sin. You never want to get between a leprechaun and a treasure."

I'd remember that if ever I had a treasure to protect. But at the moment, all I had was a lot of questions, a pub owner I liked who was in big trouble, a sister witch who in trying to help out her cousin's daughter had made things worse, and a couple of detectives who had looked at me and Kathleen as though we might be called down to the station at any moment and taken to an interrogation room. If leprechauns had killed Glyn McTavish, I had a feeling I was in deeper trouble than I had imagined.

Then I realized what Lochlan had said. "Wait. Are you telling me that if leprechauns are here, there must be a treasure in Ballydehag?"

"That's what's confusing. Ballydehag is a charming, small village, but it's not known for its wealth."

I very significantly let my gaze wander the room, which was hung with priceless tapestries like something I'd seen in a museum in Paris. That coffee machine alone would be enough for some people to kill for. On a grumpy Monday, possibly me. I knew that Lochlan Balfour was one of the richest people on the planet. One of the wealthiest vampires, come to that, and they're in a category of their own.

"Lochlan, your whole castle is one big treasure box. Do you think they could be here for you?"

He laughed at that in genuine amusement. "I won't lie to you. We've had our run-ins in the past. But I've never heard of an encounter between a vampire and a leprechaun that didn't turn out the worse for the leprechaun. So no, Quinn, I don't think they're here for me."

I remembered a couple of other locals who were also treasure-obsessed. "What about Captain Blood? And Biddy O'Donnell? Biddy's not a vampire. I know they've been stockpiling antiques to sell. Could the leprechauns have found out and want to take Biddy's antiques from her?"

He tilted his head, considering. "In a fight, I'd bet my money on Biddy over any leprechaun. Almost any other creature, come to that."

He had a point.

"I heard tapping in the bakery. I thought the new baker was hanging shelves or something but there weren't any signs of construction."

"Tapping is them searching for treasure. It's a sound unlike any other. Once you've heard it, you know it. It's like a woodpecker pecking on an old tree."

"Yes, that's exactly what it sounded like." And then I gasped. "This morning when Kathleen and I knocked on Glyn McTavish's door, I heard that sound. I thought it was a woodpecker. But now I think of it—"

"It was the leprechauns. Inside McTavish's cottage."

I pulled out the button that I'd put in my pocket and forgotten about until now. "I found this on the ground near McTavish's place."

Lochlan took the button into his long-fingered hand and turned it over. He nodded. "Handmade. Probably came off the leprechaun's coat." He handed it back.

"But why are they here? Why now?" I recalled the inside of that cottage pretty well. If there was treasure, it was well hidden. "What do the bakery and Glyn McTavish and his cottage have in common?" I asked.

The nice thing about Lochlan was that he never scoffed at what might be a stupid question. He always gave my questions careful consideration. But after about half a minute of thinking, he shook his head slowly.

"None that I know of. Except that they've both been associated with death."

I felt my face scrunch up. "Murder."

"Don't get ahead of yourself. We don't know for certain that Glyn McTavish was murdered."

"If he was poisoned by Sean's stew, I suppose it could be an accident."

"Or the poison could have been intended for someone else."

"It is a weird coincidence, though, don't you think? That the leprechauns are hanging around the very place where a man mysteriously died?"

"Oh, it's extremely suspicious, I'll grant you. And I'm not saying they mightn't have killed the man. Only that it's not their usual modus operandi. Your leprechaun baker will be a tricky fellow. He can be the life and soul of the party. You'll never find a more enjoyable group to have at a social gathering. They're wonderful storytellers, excellent musicians, and love to dance. But their greed is their downside."

When I'd walked into his bakery unannounced, I had certainly found Paddy McGrath to be quite charming.

"And what's with the tapping?"

"Well, they're little people. And they tend to be in the cellars and behind the walls searching for treasure. They're very good at sniffing out all of a person's hiding places."

"So, at least one leprechaun thinks there's treasure in the bakery?"

"He must. I don't think he's here to bake."

Apart from being super disappointed that we weren't actually going to get fresh bread, I was astonished.

"But how would they know? How would they know there was treasure hidden in the bakery? And if there was, wouldn't the former bakers have taken it with them?"

"You'd think so, but the O'Connors did leave Ballydehag in a hurry. Perhaps they didn't have time or the opportunity. Or it could be an older treasure. It's amazing how often boxes of coins are found buried in a back garden and so on. People do forget, or leave their hoards behind, or die without telling anyone where the loot is hidden."

"But how would the leprechauns know about some hidden cache in the bakery?"

"Like all creatures, from humans to vampires to," he looked significantly at me, "witches, leprechauns have their own network. Stories are told and whispered from ear to ear. Many are tall tales that are clearly foolish, but you get a leprechaun in their cups and sometimes they share too much information."

"In their cups? You mean drunk?"

"I do. Think about it. They're little folk. It doesn't take so much to get a leprechaun tipsy. And since by nature they're gregarious, they tend to talk more than they should. Spill their secrets, as it were."

My head was starting to hurt from all of this. "So, you're saying that somewhere in the world a leprechaun knew there was treasure in the Ballydehag bakery, blabbed it in a bar, and now we've got leprechauns searching the bread ovens."

"When you repeat it, the theory sounds farfetched, but essentially, that is what I think."

"And the same leprechaun, or a different leprechaun,

blabbed what? That there was treasure in that falling down old cottage? If Glyn McTavish had a bunch of money, wouldn't he have used some of it to fix up his place? And maybe buy a second chair?"

He shrugged. "A man with one chair is making it clear he doesn't want visitors."

There was that. "And Sean said he'd only delivered pub meals for one."

"By all accounts, McTavish was a hermit. But you're right, Quinn. You'd never have taken him for a wealthy man. However, don't forget appearances can be deceiving. Take my castle, for instance. I make sure that the exterior looks rundown and uninteresting. But I think you'll agree that once you're inside, it's a slightly different story."

Slightly? Talk about underselling. Inside, his castle was the most forward-thinking palace you could imagine. Lochlan had decorated with the finest art, furniture, and tapestries, which I suspected he had bought new over the centuries. However, unlike most historical castles, his place also boasted the most modern of conveniences with technology so leading edge I didn't understand half of it.

"So, you're saying Glyn McTavish might have lived the way he did to hide the fact that he was wealthy."

"It's a possibility."

"But who would do that? I mean, I get that you present a certain exterior, but once you get inside this place, you enjoy your wealth. If he had a wad of cash, he certainly didn't enjoy it."

"Who's to say how a person might enjoy their wealth? To a miser it's not the spending of the money, it's the having it that's important. Giving it away or spending it actually hurts them. Their pleasure is in looking at and appreciating their hoard. Watching it grow."

He wasn't wrong. I knew people like that. The kind that you knew had a fatter bank balance than anybody else, but they were always the last ones with their hands in their pockets. Or they always accidentally left their wallet at home when it came time to pay the bill, but they boasted about their retirement accounts and had their financial advisor on speed dial.

"And somehow someone found out."

He said, "I'm not saying that's what happened, but it's possible. And it wouldn't necessarily have been a leprechaun who spilled the beans. They have sharp ears. It could have been anyone who was talking about treasure. They'd have made sure to listen and find out what they could." He looked at me. "You seem troubled, Quinn."

"I am. I'm worried about Kathleen and Bridget. What if they get blamed? And none of us want the police looking too closely at me or Kathleen."

He nodded. "The less we have the Gardaí in Ballydehag, the happier all of us are. It was one of the reasons I chose this location. When a crime occurs, they bring them in from another town. But the way things are going, I hear talk of opening a Garda station here."

This was not good news. But, given the spate of crime here recently, if I ran the police, I'd be looking at putting a detachment in Ballydehag too. I said, "The best thing we can do is figure out who killed Glyn McTavish. The sooner that's done, the sooner the Gardaí will leave. And hopefully we'll go on peacefully, and there'll be no reason for them to open an outpost in Ballydehag."

"I thoroughly agree with you, and all my resources are at your disposal." When he said that, I knew he was serious. Lochlan had a lot of resources. "What can I do?"

I was flattered that he was asking me. And it was a no-brainer. "Can you find out everything you can about Glyn McTavish? Who was he? Where did he come from? Was there something in his past that might cause leprechauns to believe he had wealth?"

He nodded. It didn't look like any of that was beyond his capabilities.

"And we should also find out more about these leprechauns. Who are they? How many are in Ballydehag? Where did they come from? And why here? Why now?"

He said, "Searching for Glyn McTavish's roots, his history and so on will be no problem. But leprechauns will never let a vampire get close to them." He gave me a slight smile. "You'll have to take that task on yourself."

"They won't know I'm a witch?"

"Oh, yes, they'll know. But they don't fear witches the way they fear my kind." He chuckled softly. "They're magical creatures, but they have blood in their veins." He made a face. "Though not so much of it."

I didn't want to think too much about a leprechaun being a snack pack to a vampire. "Well, if a leprechaun can recognize a witch, how come I didn't recognize that the man in the bakery was a leprechaun?"

"I can only imagine it's because you haven't come across their kind before. I expect from now on you'll know them right away."

I remembered Kathleen telling me there was a new man in the bakery. Had she been testing me to see whether I would recognize him as a leprechaun? Or maybe she was just messing with me. I was having trouble telling with Kathleen.

I stood to leave, declining a second cappuccino with regret. I'd have loved to hang out all day tucked away in Devil's Keep, letting the problems of the world remain outside these thick walls. However, I also felt bad for Kathleen and wanted to help her if I could. I had no idea how Mr. Paddy McGrath and his tapping figured into Glyn McTavish's death, but his sudden appearance was clearly not good news.

Before I left, Lochlan said, "Excellent idea of yours, by the way, to read *The Picture of Dorian Gray* for book club. It's cheered our resident genius so much he seems to have recovered his wit. So thank you."

I was so pleased my plan had worked. "You're welcome. Can you all have the book read by tomorrow night?"

He chuckled softly. "If we don't, we'll have the entire novel recited aloud by its insufferable author."

By the time I got back to my shop, the lights were on. I peeked through the window and saw Dierdre happily helping a woman choose a thriller. There was only the one customer in the bookshop, so I thought Dierdre wouldn't mind if I left her there for a little longer.

But as I turned to leave, I felt a presence, like I'd stepped from the sunshine into deep shadow. And I smelled dirt.

So it was no surprise when Biddy O'Donnell sidled up to me and said in her low, hoarse voice, "I've got something for you." She hefted a cardboard grocery box and said, "Come on, ye fool. Open te door."

The last thing I wanted was this old witch inside my shop but talking to her outside on the street seemed even worse. I let her in and suggested she come up to my office. Not that I wanted her there, but I also didn't want our only customer to overhear whatever it was Biddy wanted. Because Biddy always wanted something.

She pushed the heavy box into my arms, and thanks for that, and went ahead of me up the stairs. Her horrible familiar, Pyewacket, stuck her head out of the box and hissed at me, startling me so much I almost dropped the box.

"Careful with that," Biddy said sharply.

I was huffing and my arms felt like noodles by the time I lugged my burden up the spiral stairway that led to my office and storeroom. Having been carried up the stairs, Pyewacket jumped out of the box and strutted around my space, sniffing. I was glad I'd left Cerridwen at home this morning. I had no energy to break up a cat fight. It was going to be hard enough not having one with Biddy.

The old witch hadn't improved with the time she spent above ground. She could magic herself into appearing like people she saw on TV or in the street, but with me, she didn't bother. She looked exactly like what she was. A not very clean tavern owner from the 1600s who'd been hanged. Her head wobbled and her linen dress stank of filth and mold. Straggly gray hair escaped from her greasy cap, and she was definitely short on teeth.

"What'll you give me for those?" she asked before I could set down the box.

I peered inside and felt a stirring of interest. The box held some lovely books, all in perfect condition. I'd have to inspect them to be certain but based on the leather bindings and the sense of age, I suspected they were quite valuable. I glimpsed a hardback copy of *1984*. I couldn't help myself from opening the cover. Not only was it a first edition, but it was signed and dated by Orwell. A find, indeed.

I glanced at Biddy. "Where did you get these?"

"You answer my question, missy, and then I'll answer yours."

"No dice." I crossed my arms. "I am not dealing in stolen property."

She did her best to look offended, but it was a poor job. Her old bosom huffed up and down, then she let out a gasp of outrage that ejected a cloud of breath so foul my eyes watered.

Still, I kept my gaze steady.

"Found 'em in an estate sale is what," she finally said. "Fella died, and his widow sold off his library."

Okay, that happened, and Biddy and Blood had an uncanny knack of finding such sales. "And you have a receipt?" I asked.

"A receipt? What, so you can cook something?"

Of course, receipt in her time was recipe now.

"No. A paper that proves you bought these."

She got a crafty look. "Aye. It's at the house. I'll bring it, but first tell me what they be worth?" She gestured to the box once more.

There were copies of *The A.B.C. Murders*, a Hercule Poirot mystery from 1936, and a more obscure Christie, *The Seven Dials Mystery,* from 1929. I itched to put my hands on the volumes and really study them, but I resisted. Instead, I tried to look casual. "I'll need time to value them, and we won't talk money until you can prove to me that you bought these legitimately."

"You're a hard woman, Quinn Callahan," she said, sounding stroppy. "I will return with the *receipt*."

And then, gathering Pyewacket into her arms, she disappeared. Being a witch and a ghost, she had a few extra tricks up her smelly sleeves.

I eyed the box. As much as I wanted to dig into the treasures, I first had to make sure they weren't stolen. Until Biddy could prove her story of the estate sale, I felt that there was no time like the present to get on with my sleuthing. I had to figure out what happened to Glyn McTavish without involving the Gardaí.

I could well understand why Lochlan didn't want the Gardaí setting up shop in our small town. No doubt, if they did, he'd find another castle elsewhere to do up. And I'd miss him.

Until I got myself out from under the cloud of punishment, I was stuck here. And no more than Lochlan did I want the police nosing around in my business. I was a law-abiding witch, but it was hard to explain that to a regular person, especially a cop. I'd prefer not to have to try.

If it was up to me to find out more about the new bakers, I needed a reason to drop by again. What I needed was a bakery-warming present. An excuse to go and welcome our new neighbors properly. Flowers seemed inappropriate, they'd just get in the way if there was renovation going on. Besides, I'd send flowers when they actually opened to the public.

I wandered up the high street. I could get coffees and take them over. That would be friendly and would encourage a visit. Especially if I took two coffees. Then I recalled what Lochlan had said, about leprechauns liking a drink and getting tipsy fast. Perhaps a bottle of whiskey was the perfect gift. A bottle of whiskey and two glasses!

Apart from Sean's pub, the only place to buy alcohol in Ballydehag was Kathleen's grocery store, so I continued up the street until I reached Finnegan's. It wasn't busy at this time of day. I was pleased to see that Kathleen wasn't there. One less complication and distraction. Danny, who sometimes helped Kathleen, was filling out a betting form when I walked in. He was all alone and looked very pleased to have a customer. Or, more likely, someone to talk to. She paid him for his work, but he tended to hang around when she didn't need him. If he wasn't at the pub, he could usually be found at Finnegan's.

"And aren't you a sight for sore eyes?" he said. "It brightens my day to see you walk in the door, Quinn Callahan."

Danny spent a lot of his spare time at the pub, so I imagined he could help me choose a good whiskey.

I was about to ask him to help me choose a whiskey when he said, "You've heard about the tragedy, I suppose."

My heart sank. Had someone else died because of that wretched Irish stew? Or had the news spread about Glyn McTavish's death? Before I could ask, Danny shook his head. "The health and safety people have shut the pub until further notice. People have fallen ill."

"I guess they had to shut down the pub. While they investigate."

He looked outraged. "What about my health and safety? The pub is where I go to socialize and relax. Besides, there was nothing wrong with that Irish stew. I ate it myself and look at me. Standing before you in the pink of health."

I might not have said he was in the pink of health, but he did not look like a man suffering from food poisoning. "You're sure?" I asked.

"What do you mean, am I sure? Do I look ill?"

"I mean, are you certain you had the Irish stew last night? You're not thinking of another night?"

"I believe I know what I ordered for my supper. I had the Irish stew as I usually do on a Friday."

I wasn't certain what this meant, but felt it could be significant. "What time did you eat?"

He looked at me like I might have been eating something strange. "What time did I have my dinner? Why on earth should you want to know that?"

"Please, Danny. It could be important."

He shook his head. "You Americans. Who do you think you are now? Nancy Drew?"

I smiled at the joke. "It is interesting, don't you think? That others should be ill and not you?"

I could tell he preferred to think he was stronger than everybody else, but he was willing to play along.

CHAPTER 9

"You want to know what time I ate my dinner last night?" Danny said, staring at me over his betting form.

"As close as you can remember. Everything you say could be important, Danny," I said again, suspecting he was rarely considered important.

He gazed over my shoulder at the packets of crisps and candies, all the things that grocers keep close to the till, hoping your willpower will weaken.

Finally, he said, "It was six o'clock. I like to have my dinner early on a Friday, because sometimes Sean's Irish stew runs out."

I wasn't entirely sure I could trust a guy who spent as much time on a barstool as Danny did.

"How can you be so sure of the time?"

"Well, the rugby was playing on the telly, of course. The match had to end before I ordered my dinner."

I thought, in Danny's world, that pinpointing times of the

day based on sporting events was probably as good as I was going to get. And it would be easy enough to check what time a televised Irish rugby match had finished.

"Okay, you ordered your dinner at six. Did it come fairly quickly?"

"How can I say? The usual, I suppose."

"So, five to ten minutes? Even if it was slow and took fifteen minutes, could your stew have been in front of you at quarter past six?"

He nodded. "That sounds about right."

I didn't know what else to ask him. "Did it taste like it always does?"

"Oh, Sean makes a fine Irish stew. If you've never had his, you must try it."

Not exactly what I was asking, but I was still pretty pumped that we could accurately pinpoint what time Danny had eaten his stew. The one that wasn't poisoned.

"When did you deliver Glyn McTavish's groceries yesterday?" I remembered seeing the empty box.

But to my surprise, Danny shook his head. "No deliveries on Friday. Or if there were, I wasn't asked to do them."

"Did Kathleen do them herself?"

He shook his head again. "Couldn't have. I was watching the rugby, wasn't I? She wouldn't have closed her shop."

"You're saying no one delivered groceries yesterday, the day people got sick from the stew?"

"Aye. That's what I'm saying."

Then why had there been an empty box sitting in Glyn McTavish's cottage? And if it hadn't contained groceries, what had it contained?

And now I thought I'd better get on with trying to squeeze some information out of a leprechaun. Not an activity I'd ever attempted before.

"Danny, I'm actually here to buy a bottle of Irish whiskey. Can you help with that, as well?"

His eyes lit up at that. I'd never seen him move with such purpose as he took me to the section at the back of the grocery where Kathleen kept the wines and spirits. He talked me through the whiskeys explaining about small batch, peat, the aging process, and special barrels. I'd have probably been there days if I hadn't said, "I want something decent but not too expensive."

Immediately he reached for a bottle that glowed gold when the overhead lights hit the glass. "This is a fine whiskey at a moderate price. You can't go wrong."

I thanked him, and we walked back to the till. As he was ringing it up, he peered at me with speculation in his eyes.

"Of course, whiskey isn't a libation to be drinking on your own. If you're needing some company..."

No wonder he'd looked so pleased. Now that the pub was closed, no doubt he was yearning for a drinking buddy. I quickly disillusioned him of that idea. "It's not for me. I'm buying it as a welcome gift for the new owners of the bakery. Have you met them?"

He shook his head, but I could tell he'd already heard about them. "Kathleen talked to the man. Said he's nice." He put my whiskey in a paper bag and looked quite disappointed that he wouldn't be tucking into it.

I wished him a good day, and he went back to his betting form.

I hadn't gone far, retracing my steps down the high street, when I realized I didn't have any glasses. I certainly didn't fancy swigging whiskey straight from a bottle while trading it back and forth with a leprechaun who might have killed somebody. I backed up and saw that Granny's Drawers was open and Karen Tate was behind the till. I could kill two birds with one stone, as it were, find out how her guests were doing while also buying a couple of glasses that she'd call vintage but were probably just old junk from somebody's attic.

I went in and, like Danny, she looked very pleased to see me. It must have been a slow day in the shopping district of Ballydehag. Not that it was ever exactly booming.

"Quinn! How did you make out with the foraging?"

I couldn't believe she hadn't heard. I guess she'd been too busy with her sick guests and then her shop. Quickly I filled her in on finding the dead man. Her eyes grew round as I told my story.

When I was done, she said, "And you think it was Sean's Irish stew that killed poor Glyn McTavish?" She put a hand to her chest. "Imagine if my two sick guests had ended up dead. It could have finished my B&B."

I nodded. Everyone saw this death through the lens of how it would affect them. I supposed that was normal. "How are your guests doing now?"

"Your tonic worked a treat. But they've been feeling extremely sorry for themselves and making me wait on them hand and foot all morning. I only came to my shop to get away from them." She frowned at me. "Are all American men such babies?"

I thought about it. "Mostly. Yes."

"Well, when I left these ones, they were sipping weak tea and munching dry toast, so I think they'll survive."

I explained about my errand to get glasses to take with my welcome whiskey to the new bakery owner, and she said, "I've just the thing. These are genuine whiskey glasses. Old Mrs. Moriarty was cleaning out her late mother's place and came upon them. They're no good to her. She doesn't drink." Karen put three squat whiskey glasses on the counter.

I shook my head. "I only need two."

"And I'll only charge you for two. The third one's for me. I'd love to meet our new baker."

And how had I not seen that coming? How was I going to skillfully interrogate a leprechaun with another shopkeeper hanging around the whiskey bottle? "Are you sure you don't need to watch your store?" I asked her.

She raised her eyebrows and looked around the customerless space. "And miss this roaring trade? I think the bottom line will stand it. After the morning I've had, a drop of whiskey wouldn't go amiss. I'll put my 'back in twenty minutes' sign on the front door. Anyone who needs me can call me on my mobile."

There wasn't much else I could say without appearing rude. I did the best I could to look pleased and said, "Great."

When I took out my wallet to pay, she waved me away. "We'll call the glasses my part of the welcome present." She gave the trio of glasses a quick rinse and dry before wrapping them and putting them in a paper bag. Then she put her 'back in twenty minutes' sign on her front door, and we headed for the bakery.

As we passed the butcher's, which was right before the

bakery, I kept my gaze straight ahead. But Karen must have glanced in the shop window because she suddenly said, "Rosie Higgins just glared at the pair of us." She pushed her long red hair over her shoulder. "Do you think she'll ever stop hating us?"

"Probably not."

Karen and Rosie had fallen in love with the same man, and that hadn't turned out too well.

"Do you think we'd ever be safe buying our meat there?"

"Probably not," I repeated. I hadn't set foot inside the butcher's since I'd announced to the entire village that Rosie was having an affair behind her husband Sean Higgins's back. Unfortunately, it turned out that Karen was involved with the same man. Hence Rosie's glare at both me and Karen.

"It's not that I don't like Kathleen's produce, but it would be nice to buy fresh meat from Sean Higgins. His sausages are the best you'll ever taste."

I'd have to take her word for that.

We'd reached the bakery by this time. As before, the door wasn't locked. So again, I walked in and immediately heard that distinctive tapping sound.

Karen looked at me. "He must be hard at work already. I imagine every baker has their own system. He probably likes his shelves set up a certain way."

I agreed that was probably so, even though I suspected that wasn't what the tapping noise was. The sound stopped and Paddy McGrath appeared in the front of the shop.

"Miss Callahan. How nice to see you again."

He was wearing his coat, and I noticed a button missing.

His other buttons looked very much like the one in my pocket.

"I hope we're not interrupting." I noted that his feathered hat looked very similar, if not identical, to the one I had seen earlier in the day. I introduced him to Karen and explained that we'd come with a bakery-warming gift. I pulled out the whiskey and his eyes lit up. I'd been afraid he'd claim he had too much work to do, but Lochlan had been absolutely right. Whiskey was my ticket in.

"I'm delighted to have the company. It's lonely working on your own. My wife came to inspect the premises but had to return to Dublin for a few days. Come in. Come in." And he ushered us into the back of the bakery.

Apart from the cold ovens and empty counters and racks awaiting breads and buns and pastries, there was an old pine table in a corner and four chairs. A box containing a few supplies sat on a counter. There was a sack of flour, some spices, a pound of butter and milk and eggs, but it could as easily have been the leprechaun's grocery order as the beginning of his baking supplies.

He motioned to the table, and we sat down. Karen got out the glasses, and I opened the whiskey and poured. I tried not to be too obvious about it, but I made sure his glass was fuller than ours.

His eyes twinkled as he raised his and said, "*Sláinte*."

We echoed the Irish toast and all had a drink. I struggled not to make a face as mine burned all the way down my throat and stung the back of my nose. Oh, the things I had to do in the name of sleuthing.

"What brought you to Ballydehag?" Karen asked the leprechaun. Okay, it wasn't so bad having a wingman after all.

She had started the interrogation without even knowing she was doing it.

His eyes twinkled even more, and he took another drink of whiskey before answering. “Well, now that’s a bit of a long story.”

CHAPTER 10

What was it about the Irish? Everything turned into a story. Paddy McGrath said he'd met a chap in Dublin who'd once spent time in our area. The acquaintance particularly enjoyed our village and mentioned that Ballydehag had lost its only baker.

"Well, I'm a man who sniffs out opportunity," he said, tapping his nose significantly. "I thought why not?"

If Karen was surprised that anyone would boast about our little town, never mind encourage a perfect stranger to move here, she kept her feelings to herself. Instead she asked, "And have you always been a baker?"

He took another sip of his whiskey. I wasn't sure whether he was stalling or he just really liked drinking whiskey.

"Oh, I've held many a profession in my time. I'm what you might call a Jack of all trades, master of none. But my wife now, she's a lovely baker. I really bought the bakery for her, you see."

"And your wife is waiting until your shop's ready, is she?"

"Yes. As I said, she came down to inspect the place, gave

me my list of chores, and left again. She's a few things to finish up in Dublin, then she'll be joining me full-time."

Did he really have a wife? I wasn't sure I believed anything this man was saying. There was something roguish about him. He was absolutely charming, obviously a good storyteller, and a man who enjoyed his whiskey. But could we trust what he said?

"When do you think you'll open?" asked my assistant interrogator.

Once again, I was glad I'd brought Karen along.

"Well," he said, looking up at the empty bread racks. "You don't want to rush these things. My wife will make that decision, no doubt."

"Does she have a specialty?" Karen asked.

"How do you mean?"

"A bread she's particularly known for?"

"Oh, I take your meaning now." Once more, he seemed to think deeply. "She makes a fine soda bread." Then he nodded and sipped more whiskey.

I thought a bakery that only sold soda bread wouldn't last long.

If I'm going to be perfectly honest, I was a bit squiffy, as the Brits like to say, as I made my slightly unsteady way back to my bookshop. In attempting to drink my small-statured neighbor into spilling all his secrets, I'd gone over my limit with Irish whiskey. In fairness, my limit is about as much whiskey as could fill a thimble.

Still, I didn't feel like the bottle or the time spent in the bakery had been wasted. I now had some interesting information. I wasn't sure whether it meant anything, but maybe after a cup of strong coffee I'd have a better idea. Deirdre looked a bit disappointed to see me, so I asked her if she was tired, and she insisted that she wasn't.

"I don't need much sleep," she admitted. "I never did."

Lucky her. I could use a nap right now. "Well, if you'd like to stay, I'd be really happy to have the help. I think I might go upstairs and do some stocktaking." How was that for a code name for taking a nap?

I might have felt guilty if she wasn't so genuinely happy to be able to stay among the books and the odd customer.

"But first," I said, "I'm having a cup of coffee. I don't suppose I can interest you?"

We both knew I couldn't, but I wanted to be polite. And she paused as though genuinely giving it some thought before declining my offer. I went into my small kitchen and brewed up a double-strength coffee. While I was heading back through the shop to the spiral staircase leading up to my office, stockroom, and the space where Lochlan and I run the vampire book club, the doorbell jingled, letting me know a customer had arrived. It didn't matter because Dierdre was there, so I kept going. Until a voice called my name.

"Quinn, I was hoping to catch you," the cheerful voice said.

I knew it well, but in truth it wasn't my favorite of the voices you hear in Ballydehag. Still, I pasted a pleasant smile on my face and turned to greet Giles Murray, the photographer. Giles wasn't a regular visitor to my shop, and we weren't best buddies, so if my senses hadn't been slightly dulled by alcohol, I would have probably guessed right away that he wanted something. As it was, I stood there, pretty much like a fish in a barrel looking up into the mouth of a shotgun while he came closer.

"Oh, have I caught you about to enjoy a coffee?" He left such a hopeful question mark at the end that I really had no choice.

"Do you want a cup?"

He looked as though I'd offered him a brand-new telephoto lens or something. He brightened right up. "That'd be grand."

Reluctantly I went back and made a second coffee, then hurried to settle him at one of the cozy reading nooks with armchairs and a small table between that I'd set up in my shop.

Before I could, he asked, "Is there somewhere private we could speak?"

What on earth could he want? I was certain he knew about my upstairs space. There weren't many secrets in Ballydehag. So, I led the way up to my office, trying not to slop coffee as I navigated the spiral staircase.

Fortunately, the chairs were stacked neatly in the corner, not settled in a circle like we usually did for book club, and there were boxes of stock all over the place. This space really didn't look like it was actively used for a late-night book club, for which I was grateful. I wouldn't have been so much of a stickler for tidying up after every meeting, but the vampires were always very careful to remove all trace of themselves. I suppose those instincts for privacy and secrecy were well entrenched.

I said, "I was just coming up to do some stocktaking and

bookkeeping." I hoped he got the hint that I had to work, not socialize.

It seemed like he did. "I won't take up much of your time. To be honest, I have a favor to ask you."

Well, that didn't knock me off my chair.

I sipped my coffee. It was strong enough to make me blink but still not enough to get rid of the taste of whiskey stuck in the back of my throat.

He said, "As I'm sure you've heard, Quinn, I'm working on a very exciting project. A coffee-table book of my better photographs of Irish country life. Living in the country, you can't help but come across the most fascinating characters."

Tell me about it.

"My extended photo essay, if you like, almost a love letter to the disappearing villages of Ireland, is one of the projects I'm the most proud of in my career."

"That's wonderful," I said. I had a bad feeling that he wanted monetary help for his publishing process, so I began scrambling for excuses as to why I couldn't fork over any cash.

He kept waxing eloquent about the way Ireland was changing and how he wanted to capture village life and the interesting characters like the ones we had living right here.

He laughed softly. "Of course, it's not always easy to get good photographs of our most interesting neighbors. I often have to be very persuasive." He stared at me as though I might sympathize, and I had an even worse thought.

Giles wasn't going to try to photograph me, was he? That was the last thing I wanted. Besides, I was an American transplant, hardly an Irish lass.

"I tried to get a photograph of Ballydehag's most influential citizen and largest landowner. But Lochlan Balfour turned me down in no uncertain terms."

I ha-ha-ha'd along with him with a slight hysteria edging my laugh. It wouldn't be much of a photographic coffee-table book if he tried using vampires as his subjects.

"In any case, my book's coming out in a few months. But if I'm honest with you, the advance sales aren't as robust as my publisher had hoped. By sharing some of my photographs ahead of time on social media, I've built a fair following, and my audience is growing every day. But I'm not sure my Instagram followers are pre-ordering my book."

I nodded, feeling sympathy. I saw a lot of promising books come through my shop that didn't sell as well as I'd have imagined they would. "Book marketing is tough."

"I was wondering what I could do to help with the promotional marketing, and I recalled the amazing event that you coordinated for the late Bartholomew Branson's posthumous novel."

I shuddered at the thought of that fiasco. And Bartholomew Branson might be *late* to Giles, but the only thing Bart was ever late for in my world was book club meetings. Mostly because he liked to make an entrance as he considered himself the most illustrious member of the group. Oscar Wilde, naturally, disagreed and usually managed to stroll in several minutes after Bartholomew. If anyone remonstrated, he would, of course, quote himself. "Punctuality is the thief of time," he'd say, before settling himself in a chair.

In any case, while the launch of Bartholomew's final novel had definitely been successful for book sales, it had been a stressful time for me. And I failed to see what it had to do with Giles.

He was looking at me as though waiting for me to speak, but I didn't know what I was supposed to say.

Finally, he said, "I was wondering, Quinn, if you might do something similar for my book? I can't imagine a better place to launch *Ireland through my Lens* than in one of the very self-same small villages that I am showcasing, eulogizing if you will, in my book."

I opened my mouth, but he jumped in and said, "I know you'll be stocking my book, but I've got an advance copy for you." He reached into his leather satchel and brought out his hefty coffee-table book.

I'd completely forgotten to order copies. I'd had so much on my mind it hadn't even been on my radar. But Giles didn't have to know that. I had a few months, and that was plenty of time.

I put a smile on my face, making a plan as I spoke. "Of course. I'll be showcasing your book in my front window. I think it's a wonderful thing for our village. But, other than that, I suppose I could have a little wine and cheese in the shop if you like. Invite the locals. See if that gets you more social media interest."

His eyes didn't exactly light up with my generosity. "Actually, I was rather hoping to launch my book at the castle."

I doubted very much that Lochlan Balfour would host another book launch for as long as he lived. And that was going to be a very long time.

I said, "But Devil's Keep has nothing to do with me. You'd have to speak to Lochlan Balfour."

Giles leaned back and stretched his legs out in front of him. He lifted an eyebrow and gave me a skeptical look. "I think we both know that one word from you and Lochlan Balfour would do anything."

My eyes widened. In shock, I suppose. "You think that Lochlan is...? That Lochlan and I are...?" I shook my head vigorously. "No. We're just friends."

He was still staring at me and more seemed to be required. "And I ask his advice about business." That was true. I also asked his advice on various other ticklish subjects. But romance? I wasn't going there. Not today. And not with Giles looking at me like he was.

He set down his cup, thank goodness, and rose. "I won't take up any more of your time. But perhaps you'd mention a launch party to Lochlan? Even if you're only friends..." He paused as though we both knew that wasn't true. "Lochlan is more likely to oblige you than me."

That was most assuredly true.

"I'll just leave you this little brochure with all the information about my book. You should give it to Lochlan. Let him have a look at the advanced copy. I'm very proud of my work."

I didn't know what else to say, so I agreed. My nap would now have to wait. Luckily the brochure had the publishing information, and I scrambled to order in a dozen copies of *Ireland through my Lens*. Even at a dozen, I thought I was being generous. I doubted that anyone in Ballydehag wanted to spend this kind of money on a book featuring places and people they saw every day. Knowing them, anyone whose photo was in the book would expect a free copy. Come to think of it, if my picture was in his book, I'd want a freebie too.

As it turned out, it was a good thing I was at my desk working because not five minutes after Giles left, Dierdre came in. Even though she loved to help in The Blarney Tome, I didn't want her to think I was taking advantage of her by napping during opening hours.

"I thought I'd just tidy up those coffee cups," she said in a brisk tone, though I suspected she had gossip on her mind. She looked at me and said, "And what did that poser want?"

"You don't like Giles?" I asked, somewhat surprised. I didn't even know she knew him.

"Oh, he's all right, I suppose. But he's as slick as newly polished ice, that one. And what's he doing sniffing around you the minute his girlfriend is out of the picture?"

How had I not noticed Giles was alone? Dierdre was right. He was never alone. Since I'd moved here, I'd never seen Giles without Beatrice in tow. But she hadn't been with him today, for whatever reason. "What happened to her?"

She raised her eyebrows significantly. "That's what we'd all like to know. Has Beatrice finally come to her senses and found a man her own age? He says she's just gone on holiday to visit her mother, but I'll believe that when she turns up by his side again."

"Wouldn't he say if they'd broken up?"

"Not a man with that ego. Not if the breaking up was her idea. Either way...here he is, the second she's gone, making sheep's eyes at you. The shame of him. Did he ask you out, then?"

"No," I said as sternly as I could. "And if he did ask, which he won't, I'd turn him down flat. If you must know, he wants a favor. He wants me to ask Lochlan to put on a book launch for his photographic coffee-table book at the castle. Like the one Lochlan hosted for Bartholomew."

"Well, if it wasn't a date he was after, I could have told you

Giles Murray wanted a favor. That's not a man who ever opens his mouth unless there's something in it for him."

I heaved a sigh. "What am I going to do? Lochlan will never agree."

She shrugged philosophically. "He might if you asked him."

I felt uncomfortable, as though she was going to tread conversational ground that Giles had already been over, and I really didn't want to go there.

"Well, I'm not going to ask him. I'll tell Giles I did, and he said no."

She nodded. "Excellent idea. Anyway, you know what the locals are like, if they're not best pleased with their photos, they could make a dreadful fuss. The castle's a haven of peace and tranquility. We don't need any of that nonsense."

If she thought that castle was a haven of peace and tranquility, she had a very short memory. Between the Wilde vs. Branson literary feud, and the supposed headquarters of Biddy and Blood, thieves and eBay sellers, there was never a dull moment at the castle.

Curious, I opened the coffee-table book and flipped through. I knew Giles Murray was a good photographer, but I hadn't imagined he'd be able to capture the Ireland he claimed was rapidly disappearing.

However, as I turned the pages, I found myself enjoying the photographs and seeing how he'd caught moments that might not be seen fifty or even twenty years from now. Each page held only one and beneath it was a short essay, presumably penned by Giles himself. If his prose was a little heavy-handed, his photographs were quite wonderful. There was Danny, sitting in his usual spot at the pub, whiskey in hand.

There were a pair of older women sitting knitting. I could almost hear them gossiping and the clack of their needles. There was nothing posed about the photographs. It could have been taken by another knitter who'd paused to snap a candid photo. Perhaps because they knew him, or because he'd taken time to catch the perfect image, these were tiny snatches of life.

There was Father O'Flanagan tending the roses that grew in the church graveyard. He wore an apron over his cassock. In the background was the yew tree that had helped imprison Biddy. Even though Giles could have had no idea of the magic in that tree, he'd instinctively included it in the background.

An old man dug up potatoes. Some children played at the beach. A ruined, roofless stone house. A stone cross. A céilí in someone's home, with a circle of fiddle players. None of the big local attractions were included. Not the Blarney Stone or the Wild Atlantic Way, except as a playground for children. This was an intimate portrait of a way of life, as Giles had said, that was, if not vanishing, not as prevalent as it had once been.

I was charmed. While I wasn't sure how well the book would sell here in Ireland, I imagined it could be very popular in the US, where so many people had Irish roots. I might not be able to offer him a book launch at the castle, but I could contact booksellers in the States and tell them about the project.

As I thought of the castle, I wondered that it hadn't been included. Devil's Keep wasn't a tourist attraction, but it was as active a part of this community as the grocery or the church. I flipped through the book again and sure enough, there was no photo of the castle.

Odd.

THOMAS BLOOD WAS the first to arrive for the vampire book club meeting. He came in hearty and full of good cheer. He wore his hair long and curled and preferred to dress in the costume of his time when he could. He wore a velvet jacket with large brass buttons and boots with spurs. He'd have carried his sword, but Lochlan had taken it away from him as he could be unpredictable when his temper was riled.

Lochlan came in right behind him and I could feel my tense muscles relax. I was never comfortable alone with Thomas Blood. He was definitely not as refined as most of the vampires, and he spent altogether too much time with Biddy O'Donnell.

This evening, however, he was clearly in a good mood. "Mistress Callahan," he said, making me a bow. "And how's your fine self this evening?"

"I'm good. Looking forward to our book discussion."

"And speaking of books, how are you making out valuing the volumes my colleague, Mistress O'Donnell, brought to your attention?" He nodded to where the box Biddy had brought me sat in a corner.

"I can't value them until I have proof of where they came from," I reminded him.

He shook his head. "It's a terrible thing to see such a lack of trust. Biddy's your family. She'd no more cheat you than she'd..." Since he obviously couldn't think of a way to finish that sentence because we both knew Biddy had likely killed both her husbands, it was lucky that Dierdre arrived next.

While she fussed around making sure the chairs were in a perfect circle, Lochlan quietly asked what Thomas Blood had been talking about. I filled him in just as quietly and showed him the box. He had a quick look inside and raised his eyebrows.

"They aren't yours, are they?" I asked him. I knew he had an incredible collection of books, but surely not even Biddy and Blood would be foolish enough to steal from Lochlan. I must not have been convinced because I held my breath until he shook his head.

"Not from my collection, but from a fine collection."

I repeated the story Biddy had told me about a dead collector and his widow selling off his treasures.

All Lochlan said was, "Pity I didn't hear about this sale."

I tried to stifle my yawns as the rest of the vampires trickled in. The truth was, I was exhausted not only from lack of sleep, but from the stress of finding poor Glyn McTavish's body. I was worried about Kathleen and her cousin's daughter and whether her instinctive actions to help along little Bridget's career might have brought a lot of trouble to Ballydehag.

I even wondered whether Kathleen might find herself punished as I had been. I didn't want to lose her. She was a friend as well as a sister witch, but in messing with Sean's stew, she'd done a very foolish thing.

Of course, since I was not a vampire with endless time and super abilities, I hadn't been able to read the entirety of *The Picture of Dorian Gray*. I'd managed the first few chapters and then, feeling guilty, had pulled up a summary on the internet. At least I knew the main plot points and had a pretty good idea of the writing style. He was a great writer, was Oscar, however annoying he could be in his undead life.

I'd found myself enjoying his wordplay and giggling aloud at some of his one-liners, many of which were still quoted today.

As the vampires arrived, they settled themselves in the circle of chairs. For once, Oscar wasn't late. He arrived in plenty of time, holding a gorgeous volume, which was in perfect condition and obviously very old. As a bookseller, I noticed these things.

As a treasure hunter and eBay seller, Thomas Blood also noticed. He turned to Oscar and said, "That's a fine-looking book you've got there."

Oscar glanced down as though he had forgotten what he was holding. "Ah, yes," he drawled. "My own dear words bound in calfskin. From the first print run, of course."

If Thomas Blood were a hound, his nose would have twitched, and he'd have started baying. Instead, he said in his loud, bluff way, "That'd be worth a few bob. I could give you a good price."

I, of course, had been thinking first edition and, probably like Thomas Blood, trying to calculate what a first edition of *The Picture of Dorian Gray* in mint condition would go for.

Oscar shuddered artistically. But then Oscar tended to do everything artistically. "I may have died in penury, but my fortunes have changed. I would no more sell this perfect child of mine than I would cut out my own tongue."

"Pity," said Bartholomew Branson as he strutted into the room, appearing very pleased with himself since he'd managed to be the last one in the room.

I'd wondered if he'd even show up. I could tell this was going to be an interesting meeting already.

Lochlan must have seen me yawn. "Quinn, you look tired. Is this too much for you tonight? You can go off home to bed if you'd like, and I'll make sure to lock up."

I shook my head. "I appreciate it, but I'm excited about the book discussion."

Plus, I'd seen over Lochlan's shoulder the way Oscar's face had fallen at the very idea that I might not stay. I wasn't a vampire, but maybe because of that, they tried to impress me with their discussion points on the various books we read. Oscar as well as the rest. Besides, how often did you get to discuss a major piece of literature with the long-dead author himself? I wasn't going to give up this chance.

Lochlan merely nodded and took a seat. Apart from the three copies I already had in the shop, Lochlan also owned a copy. While it probably wasn't as valuable as Oscar's own, it appeared to be a very early edition in excellent shape. And I'd been able to get some books shipped over from a nearby bookstore in Skibbereen, so everyone had a copy.

"Right," I said, looking around. "It's a real pleasure to have the author with us as we discuss this classic."

Oscar dipped his head and made a flourish with his hand as though he were a courtier bowing to a queen. Now that he was in a good mood again, he was nothing but entertaining.

There was a short silence, probably because Oscar was in the room and if anyone saw something in his book that he hadn't intended or, heaven forbid, criticized it, he would no doubt use his devastating wit to cut them down to nothing. So I imagined this was my old book club in Seattle and I was hosting.

I said brightly, "What do we think about the themes?" Then I glanced at Dierdre because she could always be counted on to say something intelligent without hurting anyone else's feelings.

She cast a quick glance at Oscar and then said, "Obviously, it's about appearance versus reality. Dorian Gray's picture collects the evidence of his sins and misdeeds, so the young man can remain perfect and beautiful. Blemishless. However, like all attempts to hide terrible deeds, they eventually came to haunt him." She opened her copy and quoted, sounding like a school teacher,

> "I am jealous of everything whose beauty does not die. I am jealous of the portrait you have painted of me. Why should it keep what I must lose? Every moment that passes takes something from me and gives something to it. Oh, if it were only the other way! If the picture could change, and I could be always what I am now! Why did you paint it? It will mock me some day—mock me horribly!"

Dierdre raised her head and said to Oscar, "It's as though you knew one day you'd become ageless."

His smile was bitter. "If I might quote myself, 'Behind every exquisite thing that existed, there was something tragic.'"

We all nodded. And then Lady Cork—who had run a literary salon in the 1700s, and presumably knew how to get a book discussion back on track—said, "Isn't your novel also about how one can turn one's own life into a work of art?"

Oscar turned to her and said, "I often think you're a great featherhead, Mary, with more silk in your gowns than you have wit between your ears, but I have to say that is very true."

As compliments went, it wasn't the best one I'd ever heard, but with Oscar, you took what you could get, and the moment of deep sadness lifted.

Lady Cork tittered and said, "But you weren't very kind to Americans, were you?" She opened her book and read.

> "Really! And where do bad Americans go to when they die?" inquired the duchess.
>
> "They go to America," murmured Lord Henry.

Lady Cork arched her eyebrows.

"If only they would," Oscar said, looking significantly at Bartholomew Branson.

I hid my laugh behind my hand.

The discussion went on and, to be honest, I didn't really follow it very intently until a voice said, "Quinn, are we boring you?

I gave a start and realized Oscar was staring at me, rather petulant. "I'm sorry. I was thinking about Glyn McTavish."

"What on earth has that uninteresting and very dead hermit got to do with my artistic genius?"

He might be worried about his artistic genius, but I was worried about a murderer loose in Ballydehag and what it could mean for all of us.

I said, "I was thinking about *The Picture of Dorian Gray* in relation to that murder."

Lochlan raised his eyebrows. "I've seen the postmortem photographs. You surely don't believe that Glyn McTavish had a portrait where he was young and beautiful hidden away somewhere? I can't imagine that man was ever beautiful, no matter how young."

I shook my head. "Not a picture of himself, but what if he had a magnificent work of art that he'd stolen, and it was hidden somewhere in his cottage? Could that be the treasure the leprechauns are searching for?"

"Anything's possible, I suppose, but wouldn't he have had the painting on display even for his own pleasure?"

I said, "You'd think so. But maybe he was so paranoid that he only brought it out on special occasions. That might explain why the leprechauns are here and tapping away on the walls. Maybe they're trying to find it."

"It doesn't explain how he was killed, though, does it?"

No, it didn't.

"If we could get back to my book now?" Oscar said with a definite whine.

CHAPTER 11

The next few days passed peaceably enough. I actually managed to get back to the business of running a bookshop. I waited in dread that the police would call and want to interview me and Kathleen further, but I was still waiting. Danny, clearly inspired by my gift to the new baker, showed up at my shop with a bottle of whiskey.

"Quinn," he said, beaming. "I thought I'd continue your education about whiskeys. Now, this one you'll find is a lighter flavor, a little heavier on the peat than the last one you tried. It'll dance on your tongue like a chorus of angels. Let me show you."

I was working in a bookshop. It was the middle of the day. And without so much as a by-your-leave, he went into my little kitchen and came back with two coffee mugs. He spun the lid off the whiskey bottle like the old pro he was and poured generous splashes into each cup.

"*Sláinte*," he said with gusto.

"I really shouldn't be drinking in the day when I'm working," I said.

"Nonsense. Just a nip to put some warmth in your bones."

A stronger woman would have put the cap back on that bottle and told him to go away, but Danny was harmless, and I knew he was bored out of his head with the pub being closed. I imagined Kathleen had grown tired of him hanging around the grocery store and told him to find another perch. Besides, the bookshop wasn't busy. I took a sip of the whiskey. It tasted like every other whiskey to me, but I listened as Danny talked about the drink as though it were a dear friend.

"It meets you quietly, like, with just a tip of the hat. And then as you welcome it onto your tongue, it warms up and fills your mouth with its personality."

I tried to find the personality of the whiskey in my mouth, but all I tasted was peat. Well, they call it peat. To me it tasted like a dirty ashtray. A whiskey connoisseur I would never be.

After I halfheartedly told him it was good, he said, "Glyn McTavish liked a good whiskey."

I was so astonished I swallowed another sip of whiskey too fast and choked. When I'd got myself under control and wiped the tears off my cheeks, I said, "You knew Glyn McTavish?"

"Well, not as you'd say knew him well. But if I delivered his groceries in the nice weather, we'd sit outside on his step and have a chat."

This was astonishing information. "I thought he was a complete recluse and wouldn't talk to anyone." I had to make certain Danny wasn't just making it up. A man who drank as much whiskey as he did might be prone to fantasies, for all I knew.

"Well, he was, and he wasn't. If it was Kathleen coming

along with his groceries, now, he'd nip in the house and stay there. I think he found her too much of a gossip."

And Danny wasn't?

He settled his elbows on my cash desk as though it were a bar and, in order to get his story out of him, I remained quiet and waited. "It all started one day when I was doing the deliveries for Kathleen. I pulled up in the van and could see him nip out of his chair where he'd been sunning himself on the front porch and scamper inside that old cottage like a frightened rabbit. I brought the groceries up to the top of the stoop and noticed a book lying open where he had abandoned it. 'You've left your book outside,' I shouted. *Angela's Ashes*, it was. By Frank McCourt. God rest his soul. And as I'd recently read the self-same book myself, I told him I had some harrowing tales, too, from when I was a lad. I thought he wouldn't come out and was about to head back to the van when he came outside and shut the door behind him. Since I packed the groceries, I happened to know there was a bottle of whiskey there. And before you knew it, we were enjoying a drink and a chat as pleasant as you please."

Danny might have been the only person in Ballydehag who'd really spoken to the dead man. He might not be the most reliable witness, but he was all I had.

"What was Glyn McTavish like?"

Danny seemed to cast his mind back. "Well, he wasn't much to look at. Thin and gray of complexion. Not much of a head of hair."

I'd seen the man. Admittedly dead, but I had seen him. I didn't need a physical description. "I meant, what was he like as a person? Was he funny? Did he have interests? Did he talk about his past or why he came here? Do you have any idea why he was a hermit?"

He shook his head at me. "Asking a man a load of questions like that isn't something you do." He sent me a sidelong glance. "Unless you're American."

I let that pass. I was still a firm believer in direct communication.

"I'd have said he was a man with trouble on his mind. He never spoke about the past, but he did love books. Well, with all that time he spent alone in that cottage, he didn't have much else to do. He'd recommend something to me and if I read it that week, we'd talk about it when I went back."

"Did you always deliver his groceries?"

"Quite often I'd offer, and Kathleen's usually happy to have the help. But, if Glyn hadn't ordered groceries that week, or Kathleen didn't need me to take them to him, I might wander out on my own."

"And he never invited you inside the cottage?" I couldn't get over that single chair sitting by the fire.

"He never did. So, I made certain only to go when the weather was good. No work of fiction is so riveting I want to sit on a cold, stone step and shiver for it."

My next question came easily. "Did anyone else visit Glyn McTavish?"

"Not that I ever saw."

That seemed to leave us at a standstill. I couldn't think what next to ask, and with all the will in the world to be helpful, Danny didn't volunteer more.

There was silence for a minute before my visitor said, "Well, then, I'll just enjoy my drink in peace. Stay out of your way while you're working. I'll leave the bottle in your kitchen in case you fancy another nip." Raising his cup to mine, he disappeared into one of the reading nooks, picking up a copy of The Hobbit on his way. He wasn't much trouble, apart from helping himself to more whiskey and asking me to brew him some coffee to go with it.

And with that, Danny treated The Blarney Tome the way he treated the pub. He had a preferred chair, and he'd sit there sipping whiskey and chatting away to whoever came in.

By the time he'd emptied his second bottle of whiskey, I decided either the pub was going to have to reopen or I was going to have to ask Danny to move on. Fortunately for the sake of our friendship, the pub reopened.

Kathleen brought the news, staring significantly at Danny now halfway through *The Hobbit*. He put down the book if anyone interesting came along who was willing to have a chat, and then he'd pick up the book and start at whatever page it happened to flip open. He said it was an old favorite, a novel he'd read many times. This readthrough was more a sightseeing trip for him.

"Danny, did you hear what I said?" Kathleen repeated, "The pub's reopened."

He looked up with a big, beaming smile. "Aye, that's grand." He finished the remaining whiskey in his coffee cup in one gulp, then politely reshelved *The Hobbit*. He even took his mug back to the kitchen and rinsed it. He was considerate like that, which I appreciated.

"I'll just pop up there then and give Sean my best."

And no doubt reclaim his favorite bar stool. I expected Sean would be delighted to have a steady customer back again.

When he'd left, cheerfully whistling, I said to Kathleen, "So, the pub's open again. What have you heard?"

She shook her head, looking glum. "Nothing. Nobody's talking. Sean still has his five-star hygiene rating, at least. He had the whole place professionally cleaned, anyway, just to be certain, and he's thrown out and repurchased every single ingredient that went into that Irish stew. I think he tossed a load of other things too, to be on the safe side."

"And it wasn't the meat that was off?" I hadn't seen the butcher shop close, so presumably the meat had tested fine.

She shook her head. "No. And some who had the stew didn't become ill, while others did. There was no rhyme or reason to it. I think myself that it must have been a mysterious flu."

Of course she did. That meant she didn't have to feel guilty for interfering with Sean's stew.

Even so, throwing away most of his pantry seemed like a sensible thing to do. But expensive for the young publican to lose ingredients on top of losing the business after being closed for so long. "I only hope this won't hurt his bottom line too much."

She beamed at me. "You're a quick one. I'll give you that, Quinn. I was thinking we might go in this evening and have dinner. Just to help Sean."

She didn't fool me for a second. She wanted to hear the gossip. And, frankly, so did I, but still I gave her a skeptical look.

"It's true, Quinn. We need to support Sean. He's a broken man."

I felt so bad for him. I couldn't get that picture out of my head of him when we'd walked into the bar and he was sitting there slumped over a whiskey like a Byronic hero running his hands through his disordered black locks.

"It could happen to anyone. In fact, it often does. The finest restaurants can have a food poisoning outbreak," I said.

"I know that. But he's taken it really to heart."

"Well, we must do everything we can to make him feel better about himself. I'll ask Karen to come along."

"We know Danny will be there, bless him for his loyalty."

"And his love of whiskey."

"Aye. I'll put the word out. See who else I can encourage to come tonight."

I nodded. "I'll do the same."

We settled into a good gossip, as Kathleen and I usually did when we got together. The door opened, and I glanced up to see Sergeant Kelly walk in carrying a cardboard evidence box. Instinctively, Kathleen and I stepped closer together. Neither of us said a word.

The sergeant burst out laughing. "What's with you two looking at me like I'm a one-man firing squad? I'm not here to arrest you."

Since that was exactly what we'd been thinking, we both relaxed.

I put on a semblance of a welcoming smile. "I doubt you're here to buy a book."

"Well, to be fair, I'm not a great reader. I'm here to return these." He came forward so we could see that inside the box were our foraging bags, complete with the sadly wilted herbs and roots we'd gathered the day we found Glyn McTavish.

"That was very kind of you," Kathleen said.

I just nodded even though I knew the foraged ingredients had been handled, and they'd be no good to us now.

I said, "So, nothing found in these bags contained the poison that killed Glyn McTavish?"

He looked uncertain as to whether he should answer. Then he said, "It wasn't poison that killed Glyn McTavish."

"What?" Kathleen and I both exclaimed at the same moment.

"I can't say more, but you looked so worried that I wanted to let you know you're off the hook. But keep what I've said to yourselves, would you?"

"Yes. Of course," I said.

"Thank you," said Kathleen.

After he'd left, Kathleen turned to me, with a grin. "I told you, and you wouldn't listen. I must have been right. Glyn McTavish must have fallen out of bed and hit his head, or he had a heart attack or a stroke. Oh, I'm so relieved. I wonder if Sean knows?" She looked ready to dash up to the pub with the news, so I put a hand on her arm to prevent her.

"First, we can't tell Sean. The sergeant asked us not to blab the news. Second, we don't know what killed Glyn McTavish, but some people still got seriously ill from that stew." I knew her relief would be a lot stronger than mine since she'd interfered with that stew, but she had to accept she'd done harm even if it hadn't led to a death.

She waved that away. "But it didn't kill anyone, did it? Besides, I still maintain they could have fallen ill from a flu bug or some such thing."

"Except that only people who ate Irish stew got sick. Anyway, it's not going to do Sean's business any good."

"I know. Don't think I don't feel terrible, Quinn, because I do. We'll make it up to him somehow. I have an idea for a spell that will encourage the bar patrons to spend a little more of their money. If they're thinking about that extra dessert, they'll order it. They'll be more likely to treat their friends to a round. That's all he needs, just a bit of extra business to make up for what he's lost."

"Don't go encouraging people to get into debt," I cautioned. Spells like that had a bad habit of going wrong. The last thing we wanted was for Sean to end up with too much money and the rest of Ballydehag to be suffering in poverty.

"I know what I'm doing, Quinn. You must trust me."

I didn't remind her that the last time she'd used magic in Sean's pub, it hadn't ended so well. I'd leave her to make that connection herself.

Before she left, I said, "None of the stuff we foraged will be any good now, obviously."

"Certainly not. Not only have too many non-magical hands touched them, but they've sat around too long and in a very bad atmosphere. We must gather new ones."

"I was hoping you would say that. How's tomorrow morning for you?"

She looked slightly suspicious. "What's the hurry?"

I couldn't explain why I felt the urge to go back to the area around Glyn McTavish's cottage, but I'd learned not to discount my hunches. "I don't know. I just want to see what's happening at the McTavish place. I wonder if the police are finished."

"They're bound to be if it was a heart attack or stroke."

I nodded. "Exactly."

CHAPTER 12

With Danny, Kathleen, and the Gardaí gone, I had the shop to myself again. While waiting for my next customer, I phoned Karen Tate to invite her to the pub that night and to make sure her American guests had fully recovered before they'd left. To my surprise, she said they were still in town, and still staying with her.

"But what do they do all day?" Ballydehag was a small village, and I certainly hadn't seen the two men on the high street.

"I told you Billy was interested in re-discovering his Irish roots," she said breezily. "I think he might be looking around at property." Then in a rush, she added, "Wouldn't it be grand if he stayed?"

I could think of few things less grand. Poor Karen. I didn't think she had the greatest taste in men, but obviously I didn't say so. She felt that going to the pub, in light of how sick the place had recently made her two guests, would be a bad idea. I wondered if she was busy spending her evenings with Billy and Jimmy, but it wasn't my business, so I said nothing.

Instead, I went to work on the online part of my employment. Since I'd arrived in town, and certainly since I'd unwillingly hosted the launch of Bartholomew Branson's posthumous bestseller, my online commerce was doing pretty well. I had discovered I had a knack for book selling, and I enjoyed it.

Lucinda, who still owned the shop, had been punished as I had been, getting sent to a distant outpost, far away from everything she knew. I guess that was the whole point.

I had been sent here from Seattle, and it had been quite the adjustment. But I was beginning to see that in punishing me, the witches council had done me a favor. I liked it here. It felt like home in a way that Seattle never had. Being a witch, I had always felt different. Now that I lived in a small Irish village where I was the only American, I was more obviously different. Oddly, it helped me fit in better. That was twisted logic, but I felt comfortable here. I was putting down roots in Ballydehag, and I felt a strange kind of pleasure in seeing the bookshop prosper.

However, I was also practical and fairly business-like. If I was putting all this work into an endeavor, I would prefer to own it.

Lucinda and I chatted secretly from time to time. Others used Zoom and Skype; we had the scrying mirror she'd cleverly left behind. I had a feeling that she, like me, was settling into her new home. I'd broached the idea of buying the business and the cottage from her, and she'd said she was open to the idea. Of course, we'd need to get permission from the same witches who had punished us, but so long as we both obeyed the rules and kept our witchy noses clean, I couldn't see why they wouldn't agree.

Anyway, I was learning my trade. Between customers when it was quiet, I studied up on my craft. I found that the market for obscure, out of print, and early edition books was pretty robust, and I had a nice little niche business going in that.

Lochlan had helped, giving me several titles that he'd had lying around. No doubt he had a Gutenberg Bible up there somewhere and a first edition Shakespeare, but I wouldn't have known what to do with those even if he'd handed them to me. However, he'd brought in a box that included some early James Joyce, first editions of Iris Murdoch, and a few Irish children's books that I'd never seen before. He refused to take any payment, and I didn't push it, knowing that he wanted me to succeed. He was a good friend like that. Also, I think in a way it was a thank-you for hosting the vampire book club and being extremely discreet about its existence.

I hadn't had a chance to have a closer look at the books that Biddy had brought in yet. That would be a good job while I waited for my next customer. I unearthed a perfect first edition of *Catch-22*, pleased to see some American classics in the box. There was *The House of the Seven Gables* by Nathaniel Hawthorne. My continuing assessment confirmed what I'd first suspected. There was a small fortune in literary classics in this cheap cardboard box. No doubt there were people in rural Ireland with collections this rich, but it was strange I'd heard nothing about an estate sale. Also, I still hadn't received any proof that Biddy and Blood had purchased these books and not stolen them.

I didn't have a safe, so I tucked the box in the back of my storeroom where no one would stumble on it.

THE NEXT MORNING, Kathleen and I made an early start, heading back to the area where we'd foraged only a few days ago with distressing consequences. Not only had the herbs and roots that we had harvested died from neglect or contamination, but unfortunately, so had Glyn McTavish.

Kathleen kept up nervous, non-stop chatter as she drove us back to the same spot in her van. I knew she was hoping we'd find everything peaceful, the crime scene tape gone along with the forensic technicians, and soon be able to put down Mr. McTavish's death as one of those random, unfortunate circumstances that happen when a man gets a little older and lives alone. No doubt he hadn't made regular visits to a doctor, and who could say how much he'd looked after his health?

As Kathleen reminded me. "You know what they say, Quinn? A man who lives alone doesn't last as long as one who has a woman to look after him."

I'd read that too. "Do you think it's true, though? And what about us? We live alone."

She shook her head. "That's different. We have sisters. Women are better at looking after each other and themselves. That's just a fact."

I didn't feel like arguing the point. We rattled over a patch of gravel, then turned into the narrow lane that led to Kathleen's secret foraging spot. I didn't know how secret it was since I'd seen leprechauns in the area. Not that I thought leprechauns were interested in herbs and potions the way we were. But what did I really know about them?

I was about to suggest she head to Glyn McTavish's first

when she said, “I’ll just drive closer to the cottage. I’m anxious to see if the tape is down.”

She was anxious to see if both she and little Bridget were off the hook. However, I was curious too. So I nodded, and we continued on our way. “Poor little Bridget’s been in a state.”

“Doesn’t she mind you calling her little Bridget?” I asked, thinking it wasn’t exactly politically correct.

“Why would she? Her mother’s Bridget, so she’s always been Little Bridget.”

“At her age?”

“She’s all of eighteen years old. What are you on about?”

Okay, something was not adding up. I’d seen a short woman walk into the pub kitchen and assumed she was little Bridget because she was so short in stature. But what if she’d been someone else?

“When you went into the pub kitchen, who else was there?”

“No one. I made sure of it before I walked in. Wouldn’t want Sean to catch me in his kitchen. He’d have a fit.”

“There wasn’t another woman there? A middle-aged woman not five feet tall?”

She turned to stare at me. “I can’t think who you mean. The only woman in Ballydehag I can think of that tiny is old Mrs. Whipple, but she’s been in a wheelchair for the past five years.”

It certainly hadn’t been old Mrs. Whipple I’d seen heading for the kitchen that night. So who had it been?

“She’s a good customer of mine, is Mrs. Whipple. Glyn McTavish was a good customer, too,” Kathleen said. “I wonder who the next owner of the cottage will be. And whether they’ll become a regular.”

It was nervous babble, and I could feel myself picking up on her anxious energy. Even as I tried to block that energy, I found myself getting wound up too. I so wanted to find the cottage peaceful and quiet, the only sign of its expired occupant being the lack of smoke from its chimney. We rounded the final bend, and Kathleen put her foot on the brake, lurching to a stop. We both stared at the crime scene tape that shivered in the breeze, like bunting at a parade.

"Well, will you look at that? Do you think they forgot to pick it up, Quinn?" she asked me, sounding far too hopeful.

No. I did not think that. And I didn't think she was so naïve as to think it either. "I think they're still working," I said.

"But where are they, then?" She made a point of scanning the area. "Where are the Gardaí vehicles? Where are the forensics people?"

"There's no one here." But that didn't mean there hadn't been, or wouldn't soon be, more experts poking around the now deserted cottage. I wondered what they were searching for. Instead of asking that question out loud, I shrugged and repeated, "There's no one here."

Even as I said the words, the cottage's front door eased open.

"Jesus, Mary, and Joseph," Kathleen said under her breath.

I think both of us were wondering whether Glyn McTavish himself, or his restless spirit, might emerge. But what we actually saw was even more surprising.

"What are *they* doing here?" she asked me, sounding outraged.

I was wondering the same thing myself. The two American men who were staying at Karen's bed and breakfast crept carefully out of the front door. They walked down the front steps and lifted the crime scene tape and stepped under it. It was almost ludicrous watching the moment they saw the van and the two of us sitting inside it staring at them. They stopped dead, then glanced at each other as though uncertain what to do next.

It was a tense moment. Luckily, Kathleen's vehicle was still running. The squatter of the two reached into his jacket pocket. Before I could tell Kathleen to shove the van in reverse and floor it, the taller one named Billy grabbed his friend's arm and said something that stopped him. Even so, I was ready with a protection shield. I wasn't going to get shot if I could help it, and I wasn't going to let Kathleen get shot either.

Billy put on a toothy grin and sauntered toward us as though we'd met in a park on a Sunday, walking dogs and carrying go-cups of coffee. He stopped at my window, and reluctantly I put it down. Only partway.

"Ladies. What a nice surprise."

I doubted very much it was a nice surprise for him. And it certainly wasn't for us. He didn't poke his head all the way inside the van, but I saw the way his gaze keenly searched the vehicle. What did he think we were up to? More to the point, what were *they* up to? Only one way to find out.

"What are you doing here?" I asked. Danny was right, I did prefer direct communication. But, in this case, it seemed to be the obvious question. I had no interest in pretending there was anything normal about this encounter.

He shrugged, looking sheepish. "Karen told us about the dude dying." He rubbed his nose as though checking to see if it had started growing yet. "I figure it's like in New York.

Somebody dies, then you know there's some real estate available. Me and Jimmy are in the area looking at property. We thought this might suit."

"You thought it might suit you to live in a one-bedroom cottage in the middle of nowhere?"

He gave a hearty ha ha ha. "Now you put it like that, maybe it's not the best idea. But we was curious."

"You know that's crime scene tape you just crossed." What was the matter with me? Why was I antagonizing him like this?

He glanced back as though he might pretend he hadn't seen the tape. Then, weirdly like Kathleen, he said, "But there's nobody here. I figure if it's an active crime scene, there'll be guys going around in jumpsuits and vans with scientists, but there's nobody here. We figured they just forgot to take the tape with them when they left."

I waited for Kathleen to jump in and say that's what she thought too, but she remained quiet. Maybe she had divined that we were in a precarious situation. Billy's 'friend' remained a few paces away, his hand hovering near his jacket pocket.

"Are you feeling better?" I asked Billy.

He grimaced and rubbed his stomach. In truth, he did look pale. "That medicine you gave definitely helped the bellyache. But I won't be eating Irish stew again any time soon."

Jimmy, I thought I remembered that was the name of the squat one, started walking slowly toward us. Once more, I was glad Kathleen had left the engine running. I tried to send her silent communication to be ready to floor it.

Jimmy kept coming. I thought if we tried to reverse the

van and get out of there, it would not end well for us. I could feel Kathleen was also on high alert. Between the two of us, we could cast some pretty powerful protection. I heard her muttering under her breath and suspected she was doing just that.

With his hand still tucked into his pocket, Jimmy stopped beside Billy. "What are you ladies doing so far from home?" He hadn't tried to make his tone or posture as friendly as Billy had.

They were as suspicious of us being here as we were of them.

When we didn't reply, Billy gave a big, fake laugh. "Don't tell me you want to buy this old place too?" He turned to his buddy and with his big grin said, "I informed the ladies here, that the best way to find good property is to check the obituaries."

Jimmy didn't seem to find that amusing. He'd never taken his gaze off my face.

I tried to swallow my nervousness. I said, "My friend and I came out here foraging for mushrooms. We were just checking to see whether the crime scene tape was gone." Always stay close to the truth when you're skirting around it.

Billy's eyes lit up. "Mushrooms, huh? I did mushrooms once. Crazy dreams I had."

I did my own fake ha ha ha. "Not that kind. These are for eating."

He made a face and put a big hand over his belly once more. "Don't talk to me about eating. Or mushrooms. There were mushrooms in that stew the other night. Remember, Jimmy?"

"Yeah." Jimmy didn't want to talk about mushrooms or

stew, and I wasn't entirely sure that he believed my story. Even though it was essentially true. Then he narrowed his eyes and looked at Kathleen. "You seem to know the area. Say we wanted to buy this old place. Who do we talk to? Who were his relatives? Who was close to the old man?"

He'd given himself away by referring to Glyn McTavish as the old man. How would he have known that? Unless Karen told him, I supposed. She wasn't the most discreet woman on the planet. Or even in Ballydehag.

Kathleen shook her head so her curls shook. "Nobody knows who his people were. There's no one to ask about his last wishes, even, or his funeral. He lived here all alone; he was essentially a hermit."

Jimmy didn't step closer, but he seemed to move in on us somehow. "Everybody's got somebody. This guy must have had too. And we'll find them."

Why did I feel like he was threatening us? Did he think we were somehow connected to the dead man?

As though our thoughts had gone down the same path, Kathleen said, "All I did was sell him groceries once in a while."

I added, "And I didn't know him at all."

Jimmy said, "Hear you found the guy. Dead."

Honestly, if Karen Tate had been there at that moment, I'd have slapped her. Who else could have told him that information?

I gave an artistic shudder. Well, not that artistic. I was feeling quite shuddery. "It was awful."

"How'd you know he was dead in there?" Jimmy asked.

Again, I reminded myself to stay close to the truth. "We didn't. There was no smoke coming from his chimney on a chilly day. It seemed odd. We only wanted to check that he was all right." I swallowed. "But he wasn't."

I had no idea whether they believed me, but Billy eased back a bit. He said, "Well, hope you ladies find some nice mushrooms. We'll head back into town. See if we can figure out who owns this place now."

"Good luck."

Kathleen carefully turned the van around, and we headed back down the lane. I can't say it was the finest piece of driving I'd ever seen, but considering how badly her hands were shaking, I thought she did pretty well.

"I'm sorry, Quinn," she said, and her voice was shaking as well. "We won't be foraging here today."

"I couldn't agree more. I want to get as far away from here as I can."

"Who are those men?"

"A couple of wise guys."

She gave a rude laugh. "Wise? They looked as thick as two bricks to me."

"Not wise as in intelligent. Wise as in connected."

"They won't have the internet out here, Quinn," Kathleen said.

I rolled my eyes. "Haven't you ever seen *The Godfather*? Or *Goodfellas*?"

"What are you on about, woman? Those men have seriously rattled you. I can't be thinking about the movies now."

"I believe they're connected to the mafia," I finally said.

She turned to stare at me before quickly turning her attention back to the road. "Well, why didn't you say so? And that lumpy thing the squat one was fingering in his pocket?"

"I'm pretty sure that was a gun."

"So we had a near escape from death, then?"

"I'm not sure. I don't think they wanted to kill us. Oh, don't get me wrong, they would have."

"Do you think they killed Glyn McTavish?"

"I think it's very possible." But something else was bothering me. "If they were sent here to kill him and they'd finished the job, why haven't they left?"

"I don't know, but in my opinion, the sooner they go back to America, the better."

"Exactly. And why did they return to the scene of the crime?"

KATHLEEN WAS TOO busy trying to keep the van on the narrow lane and herself from hyperventilating, so I didn't add another disturbing piece of information. As we bumped down the path, going faster than we ever had before, I had glanced back and saw a hat—a very familiar-looking hat on a not very tall person—emerge stealthily from the woods behind Glyn McTavish's cottage.

There was altogether too much interest in the shabby place for my liking. While I believed—like Billy did—that real estate in New York was difficult to come by, that was definitely not the case in Ballydehag. In fact, having come from the expensive real estate of Seattle, I salivated at the prices here. For what I could get for my little house in Seattle, I could buy a big place with land and a view of the ocean here. Or, which was what I really had in mind, I could buy Lucinda's bookshop and cottage. I'd come here against my will, but

I'd come to love it and was beginning to think of Ballydehag as home.

Not for one minute did I believe the New York thugs' story about wanting to buy Glyn McTavish's old cottage. So why were they still here?

And what possible connection could they have with leprechauns?

CHAPTER 13

Since our foraging hadn't turned out very well, I asked Kathleen to drop me off at the bookshop. I didn't really want to go there, but I also didn't want her asking me any questions if I had her drop me where I really wanted to go next. I had some sleuthing to do, and I wanted to do it on my own. I also needed to get permission from a certain vampire before I used his name, possibly in vain.

Kathleen seemed perfectly happy to drop me off and quite anxious to be on her own way. Probably, she wanted to put this whole morning behind her and pretend it had never happened. I perfectly understood how she felt.

After I'd hopped out of her van and waved goodbye, I didn't go into my shop. It was early yet. Instead, I unlocked my bicycle from the stand and rode to the castle. Since I was well known there, they let me in right away. I'd barely got inside when Lochlan came down the stairs into the lofty gallery where I was waiting.

This was where we'd held the launch party for Bartholomew Branson's last book. It was a magnificent space full of amazing tapestries and gleaming antiques, but it wasn't cozy. Lochlan kept the cozy for the parts of the castle that the public never saw. As he came down the stairs toward me, he looked like a dark angel. He wore black trousers, a dark gray turtleneck sweater, and black shoes. His blond hair glinted in the light. His ice-blue eyes warmed as they saw me.

He said, "Quinn. You look troubled."

I let out a spurt of disbelieving laughter. "Troubled? I was nearly killed this morning. Troubled doesn't even begin to describe how I feel."

All warmth and softness were suddenly gone, and he was at my side so fast I hadn't even seen him move. He touched my shoulders gently. "Are you hurt?" He scanned my body. "Do you need a doctor?"

"No. I'm not hurt. Just scared. And rattled." I quickly told him what had happened.

His eyes grew stormy. "And they threatened you? These troglodytes?"

"They didn't exactly threaten us, but they definitely wanted us gone."

"Shall I get rid of them for you?"

I didn't think he meant kill them, but I didn't want to push it. "No. I want you to ask one of your trusted vampires to keep an eye on them. Follow them if possible. What are they up to? What do they want in Glyn McTavish's cottage? If they were sent to Ballydehag to kill McTavish, then why haven't they left yet?"

He nodded once. "Consider it done. I haven't reported back about Glyn McTavish as I've nothing useful for you. I've looked into him, but he has—or rather had—almost no presence. That in itself is suspicious. He had a modest bank account in Ireland. Lived frugally. Paid his bills on time. Had no social media presence." He looked shocked. "Quinn, the man didn't have the Internet."

"What about his history? Background? Where did he come from? Did he have a job? Was he retired? Independently wealthy?"

He shook his head. "I couldn't find anything. It's as though Glyn McTavish sprang into existence when he appeared in Ballydehag eight years ago."

"I thought everyone could be tracked by technology these days."

"That's what's so curious. I suspect our Glyn McTavish was someone else in the past."

Well, that was frustrating. "Any idea who?"

"Not yet." He grinned at me. "But I do enjoy a challenge. One has so few these days."

"How long do you think it will take you to figure out who he really was?"

"A day or two should do it."

"Wow. You're good."

"Would it be bragging if I said I, and the staff I hire, are the best?"

I tried not to laugh. "Not if it's true."

"Well, it is. What else can I do?"

I let out a breath. When I'd thought about my idea on the way here, it had seemed a simple request. But now I felt weird asking him.

I said, "Could you look dangerous and threatening? If you had to?"

His stern look immediately disappeared. His ice-blue eyes

lightened in something like laughter and his lips quirked. "I think I could manage it. If I *had* to."

"I need to pry information out of those leprechauns. After you told me they're frightened of vampires, I thought I might..."

He finished the sentence I was reluctant to complete. "Voice the threat of me to get them to talk?"

"It sounded better before I told you about my plan. Are you offended?"

He paused as if to think about it. "Not really. We currently do a good job of hiding who we are. The old ways are long behind us. It might be rather nice to terrify somebody for a change."

I was glad I hadn't insulted him because, in truth, I believed he could be quite frightening if he wanted to.

"Okay, then. Could Dierdre watch the bookshop for me this morning? I need to interrogate some leprechauns before lunch."

"Do you want me to come with you and help terrify them?" He seemed quite pleased by the idea.

I considered his offer, then shook my head. "I think Paddy McGrath might talk more easily if the thought of the threat of you is there rather than you actually being there. If that makes sense."

"It does. I'll make sure I'm close by, though, in case you need me."

"I'll call your mobile if I need you."

His lips quirked again. "No need for a phone. Just speak the words, and I'll be there."

And I thought I had some powers.

I headed off once more, confident that I didn't need to

worry about the bookshop. I cycled home, put my clothes in my cottage's washing machine, and showered. I wanted to get every vestige of this morning's horrible encounter flushed down the drain. And then I dressed in clean clothes and meditated to get rid of all the chaotic thoughts. When I felt calm and centered, I cast a circle. From nowhere, my familiar appeared. I was grateful to have her with me inside the circle. Cerridwen always deepened my magic.

I focused on the white candles I'd put in the circle around me and the wicks sprang to life.

I sat cross-legged. Cerridwen settled daintily on my lap, her eyes half open, watching the candle flames. I felt her spirit mixing with mine.

"Candle white to light my path.

And get the truth from Paddy McGrath.

May I strip the truth from any lie.

And find its wisdom with my inner eye.

As I seek the truth to see.

As I will, so mote it be."

I closed my eyes and breathed deeply, feeling Cerridwen's warmth, and pictured a small Paddy McGrath in front of me speaking truth. While that vision was fresh, I closed the circle and moved my reluctant familiar. Cerridwen might be magical, but she was also very happy to snuggle up and nap.

She was also partial to tuna treats.

I left her munching away and pedaled my bicycle back to the town's high street. My legs complained. I was getting in a fair bit of extra exercise today.

This time Paddy McGrath's bakery was locked. Not so friendly and open as before, I noticed. I knocked sharply on the door.

There was a long pause where I suspected the leprechaun was checking to see who was there and pondering whether he could get away with not opening his door.

In case he decided on the coward's route, I knocked again and called through the door. "Mr. McGrath? I know you're in there. I'd like to talk to you."

I kept my voice friendly and non-threatening, but I also made it clear I wasn't leaving. A minute later, the door opened to reveal Paddy McGrath wearing an expression of delight.

"Mistress Callahan. What a pleasant surprise. Don't tell me you've come with another welcome present."

I smiled down at him. "I'm afraid not. There's something I need to ask you. Could I come in?"

He shifted from one foot to the other, peering behind me as though he might find an excuse not to invite me in. I stood firm, waiting.

Finally, he said, "I'm very busy today."

"I won't take up much of your time. It's important."

He sighed and stepped aside. "Well, you'd better come in, then." He was still wearing his feathered hat, and I was positive it was the same one I'd seen bobbing through the undergrowth this morning.

As soon as I'd entered, he shut the door sharply, then very deliberately locked it again with a loud snick. "Now then, what can I do for you?"

He didn't offer me a seat, but I led the way into the kitchen anyway and sat down. "Why don't you sit?" I said to him. There was a question on the end, but it was pretty clear I was all but ordering him.

He began to look uncomfortable. "What's this all about?"

He did as I asked, though, and sat. With the old, well-worn pine table beneath my hands, I felt more grounded. Once more, I centered myself and silently asked for clarity and the ability to see through lies to truth.

Then I just went straight for it. "What were you doing at Glyn McTavish's cottage this morning?" I asked.

He looked startled. "I've been here all morning," he said, his gaze slipping away from mine as he glanced away.

"Mr. McGrath, I saw you."

He was getting really jumpy. "What were you doing up there, then?"

"I asked you first." Yes, I actually said that.

"I was on my own business."

"Paddy, a lot of people are showing interest in that cottage. I need to know why."

"I don't know what you're talking about, young lady, and I've a great deal of work to do."

He shot to his feet, and if he'd been a taller man, it might have been quite dramatic. As he only came up to my shoulder when we were both standing, it didn't have quite the impact he'd probably hoped. I remained seated and looked him straight in the eye.

I thought about how threatening the two wise guys had been just with body language and hints of violence. For all I knew, that was nothing but a banana in the wise guy's pocket, but he'd made me believe it was a gun. Okay, I was pretty sure it was a gun. I had to do the same thing to Paddy, make him nervous and on edge without actually having a weapon or any notion of hurting him.

So, I stood up now and loomed over him. "I know who

you are. I know you're searching for treasure. I want to know what it is and where it is."

He was so stunned that he jerked his head back and his hat fell off, revealing reddish-brown hair curling close to his scalp.

"I'm sure you do. I'm sure we all do," he said with a titter.

That wasn't very helpful. "So you believe there is treasure in Ballydehag."

He shrugged. "Well, I did. Now I'm not so sure."

"But how did you hear about it? Why Ballydehag?" When he opened his mouth, I raised my hand and extended my pointer finger as though I were a teacher and he were a naughty pupil. "And don't give me any nonsense about being a passionate baker. I know you're here for treasure."

He rubbed his chin with his small hand. "And what be you here for, mistress? I doubt it's to sell books to these barely literate villagers."

I really wanted to laugh at that. It was not only old-fashioned but kind of true. However, I kept my countenance. "That's neither here nor there. I need to know about you."

"Why? So you can pinch the treasure for yourself? You're a witch, so can't you cast a spell to find where it is?"

"You know perfectly well I can't. I could probably cast a spell to turn you into something even more unfortunate than you already are, though. A toad. A rat. A dung beetle." I wasn't at all certain I could do any of those things.

"There's no need for insults. You just go about your way and mind your business, and I'll mind mine."

"It's not that easy. I'm not the only one who needs to know the treasure's location. Lochlan Balfour sent me. And Lochlan Balfour, as I'm sure you know, is a very old, very powerful vampire." I let a beat of silence pass. "And he's very hungry. He tells me that while your kind aren't a full meal, you make a rather tasty snack."

I couldn't believe I was saying these awful things. The compassionate part of me wanted to soothe the little man who was clearly becoming nervous and agitated. His eyes were darting around as though expecting the tall blond vampire to loom up behind him any second, fangs bared.

"Now, there's no need for that. I've indeed seen you in league with the powerful forces of darkness. You play a dangerous game there, mistress."

"Be that as it may, Lochlan and I are working together. You need to tell me everything you know."

"And if I don't?" It was a pathetic effort at bravado as his voice shook slightly at the end.

"Lochlan wanted to come with me, but I told him not to. He's outside. At my slightest call, if I so much as whisper his name, he'll instantly appear in this kitchen." I drew in a breath as though about to summon the vampire.

The leprechaun raised his palms quickly. "No need for that. No need for that." He let out a breath and sat back down. He motioned me back to my seat, so I re-settled myself on the hard wooden chair.

He dropped his head in his hands, assuming a posture of absolute dejection. "It never goes right for me. Never. Other leprechauns are dancing jigs upon their mounds of gold coin and treasures. But me? I always get there when the treasure's already been dug up. Or the loot turns out to be fool's gold. Aye, that's all I am—a fool of a leprechaun. Even my wife despairs of me. We probably will have to run this bakery just to make ends meet. I'm an embarrassment to my kind." He looked so pitiful I felt my heart stir, but I had to be firm.

"I'm very sorry to hear that. However, I still need to know what's going on at Glyn McTavish's cottage. What is so interesting to you? And how did you find out about it?"

He released a huge sigh. "Very well. Not a bit of good will it do you. I've looked and I've looked, and there's nothing there."

"What were you looking for?" I was really getting tired of this interrogation. How people did it for a living, I had no idea.

"I suppose I might as well tell you." He slumped back. "I like a drink, as you may have noticed. I was in Dublin at a little pub I know, and I got chatting to a sullen young man. I could sense he had trouble and, as you may know, people with troubles who are in the drink often have secrets to tell, and sometimes they can be profitable. So, he turned out to be Ballydehag's baker's son. He said they'd had to depart the bakery in a hurry and leave everything behind. He swore there was money still here. I assumed he meant his father, the baker, had hidden funds. Many people do, still, you know. There are strongboxes inside walls, cleverly concealed safes. Money stuffed in cookie jars and under mattresses. If they'd had to leave suddenly, I thought why not come and find the loot? My wife told me I was being a fool." He glanced up. "She tells me that often. And I probably would have forgotten all about it, except that a few days later, in the very same pub, in fact, two American fellows walked in." He glanced up at me. "Accents like yours, mistress. Though, I'm sure you won't mind me saying this, not quite so refined."

I nodded to let him know I didn't mind him saying that at

all. "Was it the two New Yorkers who are in Ballydehag now?" It seemed the obvious conclusion.

He nodded. "It was indeed. They were just off the plane, they said. Came in for a Guinness. Well, the squat one, he can keep his tongue between his teeth. But the taller one, you get a few drinks into him, and you can't shut him up. Naturally, after the Guinness, they tucked into the Irish whiskey. Between that and the lack of sleep on the airplane, the tall one became quite garrulous. And loud. It was he who mentioned Ballydehag and paying a visit to Glyn McTavish. He said to his friend, 'When we take back what he stole, Big Al will take care of us, don't you worry.'"

"Who's Big Al?"

"Their employer, I assume. They both seemed quite nervous of Big Al, whoever he might be."

"Interesting. Did they say what they were here to collect?"

"Of course not. If they had, don't you think I'd have found it afore now? I'd managed to sidle up on a barstool as close as I could to them, hoping to hear more, but after a while the squat one yanked the other one out of the pub and told him to go sleep it off.

"I went home to my wife and told her we were making a new start in Ballydehag. She wasn't best pleased with me, but she agreed to give it a try. Dublin hasn't been so good to us. Very difficult to make a living there. And it only gets worse with the debit and credit cards. Nobody carries loose gold anymore. It's a tragedy."

A tragedy for him, maybe. Pretty convenient for those of us who didn't want our gold stolen, though.

"And they definitely said they were coming to find Glyn

McTavish? Going to his cottage?" This puzzled me as much as the leprechaun in front of me.

"Aye, mistress, at first they did, but then they called the man they were looking for by a different name. Glen Morgan, it was. And it was only when I got here and followed them, that I saw where they were going. There is no Glen Morgan in Ballydehag. Believe me, I've searched. But apart from showing an interest in that nice woman who runs the bed and breakfast, and your fine self, and the pub, the only place they've been is to Glyn McTavish's."

"So you've been following them?"

"Not following, exactly, but trying to keep an eye on where they might be."

"Did you see them go to Glyn McTavish's cottage the night he died?"

He looked shifty again. "I wouldn't want to get myself in any trouble, mistress. I've seen you talking to the police. The Gardaí and I don't mix."

"I won't tell the Gardaí anything you tell me. But I really need to know."

He remained silent.

I felt terrible doing it, but I said, "Why don't I ask Lochlan to come in? I'm sure he'd like to hear what you have to say—or not say."

He put a hand up in the air. "All right. Calm down with ye. I'm thinking."

"You don't have to think very hard to know whether those two men from New York were at Glyn McTavish's cottage the night he died."

"You're right, mistress, they were."

Finally, we were getting somewhere. "What time was this?"

"I don't know. I don't wear a watch upon my wrist, nor have one of those newfangled phones you people carry, clutching them to you like newborn babes. I went up just after sundown. Took a bottle of whiskey with me. Thought I might knock on his door and start up a conversation. The two men were in the pub with you and the nice woman who runs the gift shop and bed and breakfast."

"Karen Tate."

"Aye. While the New Yorkers were engaged with you, it seemed a good opportunity to have a quiet chat with the man himself. Glyn McTavish, or Glen Morgan, as it might be. Maybe have a little look around his home."

"After sundown?"

"Aye," he said again.

Okay, I could work with that. I checked Google on that precious phone I carried around like a newborn babe and found out soon enough when sundown had been the night Glyn McTavish died. "Sunset was just before eight o'clock."

"Sounds about right."

"And did Glyn McTavish see you? Did he let you in?" I couldn't imagine it, but he'd made friends with Danny, so maybe.

"When I knocked on his door, a harsh voice asked, 'Who's there? What do you want?' As politely as I could, I said I was new in town and wished to introduce myself. I told him I had a bottle of nice whiskey with me." He shook his head looking sad. "Maybe I should have bought better whiskey. He told me to go away."

"And did you?"

"Not immediately. Seemed a shame to waste the whiskey. And the night was fine. I sat on his front porch, didn't I? Pulled out my pipe. Thought if he saw me sitting there, Mr. McTavish might care to join me."

I could just imagine him, too. Sitting on someone else's porch, helping himself to their chair, stretching his short legs out in front of him and crossing them at the ankles. I bet it was a corncob pipe in his mouth. In my vision of him, it was.

"I sat there for a little while, nothing much happened." He looked at me confidentially. "I really should have bought a nicer bottle of whiskey. Especially if I'd known I'd be drinking it by myself." He seemed to go back in time.

I remained silent, letting him wander down memory lane at will.

"It grew dark, and I thought I'd wait until the man was asleep and let myself in to have a little look around. Before I could, I heard the sound of a vehicle approaching. I didn't know who else was coming to visit, but just in case they weren't any more fond of visitors than Mr. Glyn McTavish, I made myself scarce."

"You went home?" That was a lame ending to his tale.

He looked quite offended. "No, I did not. I tucked myself on an old stump at the edge of the woods. You wouldn't know I was there unless you shone a light directly on me, but I had a good view of the door and of the lane leading up to it." He shook his head.

"I know exactly where it was," I said. "You lost a button there." I reached into my pocket and pulled out the button I'd brought along, in case I needed to remind him of where he'd been that night.

He looked happy to see the button again.

"I'll tell you this, the person driving didn't much know what they were doing. I think perhaps they were unaccustomed to a stick shift. The car seemed to kangaroo along on the wrong side of the road. Lucky for the driver, there was nothing coming or there'd have been a collision. After a while it came to a stop and the two gentlemen from America got out. Up they swaggered to the front door, just where I'd been, and banged their fists on the door. Not pleasant like I'd been. Angry, like."

"Then what happened?"

"He must have told them to go away as he had me. I didn't hear the words, just his voice. And he didn't open the door. Next thing, the squat fellow yelled out in a menacing tone, 'Glen Morgan, we know you're in there.'"

I felt my throat constrict. I could only imagine how frightened poor Glyn McTavish, or Glen Morgan or whatever his real name was, must have been inside that cottage. Where would he go for help? Who could he call?

Now that Paddy McGrath was in the middle of telling the story, he seemed to relish the drama.

"Nothing happened for a minute. Two minutes. And then they banged on the door again. This time I heard the man inside yell, 'Go away. I'm calling the Gardaí.' The tall one laughed. 'I don't think so. Or we'll tell the cops who you really are. You're probably wanted in Ireland as well as the States. Now just open the door, and we'll talk this through. Nobody needs to get hurt.' It looked to me like they both had guns in their hands. You know, the short, blunt ones like you see in the movies."

"Handguns?"

"Aye. I think so. I had my hands over my ears waiting for

the bang as they shot the lock off the door, but suddenly it opened. And there stood Glyn McTavish, or Glen Morgan, as I assume. He just looked like an ordinary old man wearing pajamas and a bathrobe. He stepped aside, and they walked right inside and shut the door."

He seemed to think back. "Oh, wait. Before that, the tall one said to the squat one something I thought was very strange."

"What's that?"

Paddy McGrath looked at me. "He said, 'You got the wrench?'"

"You got the wrench?" I repeated, to make sure I'd heard it correctly.

"Yes. It didn't look to me like they were there to fix anything."

"How weird. I wonder if it was some kind of code? Like a password?"

"Well, Glyn McTavish did open the door. But he didn't look very happy to see the two men who were standing there."

I thought if I'd opened my front door to two men with guns, I wouldn't be very happy to see them either.

"And then what happened?"

"Nothing. I sat there a little longer. And then it occurred to me that I wouldn't be visiting Glyn McTavish that night. And if those two men came out and found me, I'd be a very sorry fellow. So, I recapped my whiskey and slipped away home. Well, away to the bakery. It's all I've got for a home now."

"When did you next return to the cottage?" I could see

him about to lie and said, "I know you did, so keep telling the truth, and I won't need to call my vampire friend."

He glanced at me and looked uncomfortable. "The next day."

I nodded. At least in this, I could be sure that he was telling the truth, as I'd seen him.

"You went in and searched for treasure while poor Glyn McTavish was lying there dead."

He got a bit huffy at that. "It wasn't like I could bring him back to life, now was it?"

"How did you know the two men hadn't already taken the treasure?"

"I didn't. But I'm not a man who gives up until I'm sure there's nothing left to find."

"What did you find?"

He looked very sorry for himself. "Nothing at all."

CHAPTER 14

After I left Paddy McGrath in the bakery, I didn't know what to do with my new information. Well, there wasn't that much new information, but it did look suspiciously as though the two Americans had done away with Glyn McTavish. Whose real name likely wasn't Glyn McTavish.

I checked on Dierdre and found her happily cleaning all the cookbooks and replacing them neatly on the shelves. She held a feather duster in her hand. When she saw me, she wrinkled her nose. "They get so dusty, the books, don't they?"

I agreed they did and thanked her for her housework. I'd have felt bad, but she was so obviously enjoying herself. And she was right. The books did need regular dusting and reshelving, and when I told her I was going to pop back to the castle to see Lochlan, she just smiled and told me to have a good time.

I got another mile of biking in by pedaling up to the castle once more.

If I was going to have to keep hanging out at the pub for information, I was going to need all the exercise I could get.

When I pulled up, Lochlan himself stepped out of the door to greet me.

I said, "I wasn't sure you'd be here. I thought you were going to hang around by Paddy McGrath's."

"I did. When you left, I left."

I felt a bit chagrined. "But I rode my bicycle here. I should have beaten you."

Once more, he looked amused. "But you didn't."

I really didn't need to know.

"Can I come in?"

He opened the door, and we both stepped into the cool, dim, stone entrance hall. Then up the stairs to that lofty gallery where we'd held Bartholomew's book launch party. It had huge fireplaces where you could roast oxen. Naturally, they weren't in use these days.

He must have seen me shiver, for he said, "Come upstairs where it's warm."

Since I knew he kept it warm for me, I happily followed him up the stairs and into his private quarters.

"Coffee?" he asked.

"Oh, yes, please."

He even had biscotti to go with the cappuccino. I happily dunked and chewed while trying to sort my thoughts into some kind of order. Finally, I told him, as close to word for word as I could remember, what Paddy McGrath had told me.

Unlike me, Lochlan focused on the fact that the New York thugs had been in the cottage after Sean's Irish stew had arrived and while Glyn McTavish was still alive. I doubted very much that he was still alive when they left him. But how to prove it?

When I gave him the name Glen Morgan, he looked disappointed. Almost annoyed, the way someone gets when you tell them the end of a movie they haven't seen. Or the answer to a quiz clue they're working on. "I'd have discovered that in a day. Maybe less."

"I know. But a nosy leprechaun is nearly as good as a worldwide tech network, it turns out."

"Rarely." He pulled out his phone and started tapping. "Now we have a name, I'll be able to find out who this Glen Morgan was and why he turned himself into the Ballydehag hermit, Glyn McTavish." After Lochlan issued his instructions to whatever minions he had waiting for the task, I wondered if we'd receive the answer too late.

I said, "I'm worried those two thugs will board a plane to New York and get away scot-free. They'll get away with murder."

Lochlan tapped his long, white fingers on the arm of the chair he was sitting in across from me. "And yet, why haven't they gone? Why are they still hanging around?"

I answered the obvious question. "Because whatever they came for, they didn't get."

"Right. So, killing Glen Morgan wasn't their mission."

"Do you think your researchers can figure out what those thugs and their boss, Big Al, wanted by looking at who Glen Morgan was?"

"When we link Glyn McTavish and Glen Morgan, we'll find our answers." He looked quite eager to find them. I suspected that once Lochlan Balfour put his incredible resources to work, whatever secrets Glen Morgan/Glyn McTavish had hidden, they were about to be dug up.

"Do you think I should tell the Gardaí about Billy and Jimmy? Maybe they could hold them or even interrogate them and find out why they killed that poor man."

His face went cool and remote, and while I knew he was considering what I'd said, I could tell he was against the idea. I completely understood. He didn't want the Gardaí poking around in Ballydehag any more than I did. But justice was justice.

"I think it's unwise for many reasons, but I also don't think any police will listen to you. What do you have to go on? A leprechaun's word. They'll either laugh you out of the police station or have you sectioned for a lunatic."

"I know you're right, but I can't bear to think of them just getting on a plane and going home. Then beating up and killing New Yorkers. Every criminal we take out of circulation seems like a good thing to me."

"But we don't have any proof that they killed the man. Let the Gardaí officers and detectives do their job."

"Do you think they'll find out who killed Glyn McTavish?"

"Probably not. But you never know. We should give them the chance."

"I suppose you're right. But in the meantime, you will let me know what you find out about Glen Morgan?" I asked.

"You'll be the first person I tell." Then he said, slowly, "You know, treasure isn't always money. Isn't always gold. There are many ways to hold one's wealth."

I imagined he knew all about that.

"Are you saying that Glyn McTavish had, what? A Swiss bank account?"

He made a dismissive motion with his hand. "A Swiss bank account isn't what it used to be. Nor are offshore holdings. I was thinking more of cryptocurrency."

My eyes opened a little wider. Okay, I'd heard of bitcoin. Who hadn't? And more and more I seemed to hear about people investing in it or buying cars with it. But I didn't personally know anybody who had cryptocurrency. At least, I didn't think I did.

"Poor Paddy McGrath. He can tap away for the rest of his life and never find the treasure if it's in cryptocurrency."

"Unless he can find the password. Otherwise, Glyn McTavish's treasure was well hidden. And it might die with him." He shrugged elegant shoulders. "They'd have been better with a wrench than guns."

I felt my eyes bug open. "Paddy said, before they went into Glyn's cottage, that one asked the other if he had the wrench. It seemed so random, I forgot all about it."

Lochlan shook his head. "Not random at all, Quinn. In crypto circles, they call it the five-dollar wrench attack. People who own crypto are warned never to go down to the pub and boast about their holdings or drive around in a flashy car with stickers or license plates advertising that they're a bitcoin enthusiast. Because, even though you may have the most secure password in the world locked in your head, all it takes is a good attack with a five-dollar wrench and you'll be spilling all your secrets to the person holding the wrench."

I swallowed sudden nausea. "That's what the New York

thug meant, wasn't it? When he asked, do you have the wrench?"

"I would imagine so. Not that they had an actual wrench, but that they'd beat the man until he gave up his password, not shoot him."

I thought about it some more. "But if they had Glyn McTavish's password, I have to ask, again, why didn't they leave? Couldn't they retrieve his cryptocurrency from anywhere?"

"They could. So long as he did give them his password."

I felt so puzzled my head was hurting. I rubbed my temples. "None of this is making any sense. Remember, Kathleen and I found him. He didn't look beaten up. In fact, we first thought he'd fallen out of bed or died of a heart attack or something. Then, later, we thought he was poisoned by Sean's stew."

He nodded. "I found a copy of the forensics report. The police coroner says he died of a blunt trauma blow to the back of the head."

"You think the thugs hit him too hard?"

He shook his head. "They'd never have been sent all the way here if they weren't the best. No. Something went wrong."

I took another sip of coffee and it hit me. Not the coffee but— "The stew." I exclaimed, realizing that the bad stomachs of his attackers may have saved Glyn McTavish a beating. "They both got really sick from eating Sean's Irish stew. Wanna bet it hit them as they were about to interrogate Glyn McTavish? Pretty hard to beat on someone when you're as sick as they were."

He looked amused. "You think they left before they could get to work on him?"

"It fits with what we know. We know they arrived and that Glyn McTavish let them in. And we know that later they were very sick, and we know Glyn McTavish wasn't beaten."

"It's a...reasonable guess," he said slowly.

"It's an excellent guess," I replied. "And the thugs haven't left because whatever Glen/Glyn stole from Big Al is still hidden." I was putting my theory together even as I was speaking. "So, assuming you're correct, and they aren't digging up a box of gold in the backyard, but some kind of bitcoin password, then if they don't have it now, how are they going to get it?"

And wasn't that the multimillion-dollar question?

CHAPTER 15

I felt so confused. I had a treasure-hunting leprechaun who couldn't find a treasure. I had food-poisoned thugs who couldn't manage to beat up a mark. And a dead man whose murder was still a mystery.

"They must have killed him. Who else would have done it?"

Lochlan looked at me. I could see he didn't believe me. "If they couldn't manage to rough him up a bit, where did they get the energy to deal him a deadly blow? And why would they? The whole point of the wrench technique is not to kill but to hurt and frighten and coerce."

"Could Glyn McTavish have fallen and accidentally bashed his own head in? Maybe he was so frightened that he tried to run away and fell." Even as I said the words, I knew I didn't believe them. I kept thinking.

"And, how did Big Al find Glen Morgan who'd turned himself into Glyn McTavish? After so many years? He couldn't have been more secretive or more disconnected from the world."

"I've been wondering about that myself. He'd been so careful. How did he give himself away?"

I stood, feeling invigorated. Also quietly furious. I was proud to be an American, and I felt like I represented my country here in Ireland. Well, in this tiny corner of Ireland. I did not appreciate a couple of wise guys coming in and causing trouble. If they'd been Irish, that was one thing. But Americans? I'd had enough of it.

I said, "Lochlan, I need your help again."

"You're not going to terrify that poor leprechaun again, are you? I'm not sure he'll survive another go."

I really didn't think I was that scary, but I shook my head, anyway. "Oh no. This time I'm going to the source. I'm going to confront the American thugs."

He stood up immediately. "Well, you're not going to confront them alone."

I grinned at him. "I'm glad you said that. I was hoping you'd come with me."

"Any idea where they are?"

"Let's try Karen's place first as it's closest. If they're not there, they'll be at McTavish's cottage."

Since I'd ridden my bicycle over, I didn't have my car. So we went in Lochlan's Range Rover. It was the fanciest Range Rover I'd ever seen, with a luxury interior that included a fridge where I helped myself to a bottle of cold water. This sleuthing was thirsty work.

It wasn't a very long drive to Karen's and as we drove past the yew tree that had once held Biddy in place, I couldn't help but wonder what my annoying ancestor was up to. I hadn't seen her since I'd asked for proof she'd come across those books honestly. No doubt she was up to something. And definitely something not good.

I said, "Have you seen Thomas Blood lately?"

"Not any more than I have to." He felt the same way about Blood as I did about Biddy. "Why do you ask?"

"I just have a bad feeling that he and Biddy are up to something neither of us would approve of." I told him about the mysterious book delivery and the lack of any evidence they'd been purchased.

"I wish they'd take their thieving ways and dubious business and move somewhere else," he said.

I heartily agreed with him. By this time we'd reached Karen's bed and breakfast. I felt we were in luck as there was a rental car in the driveway. Lochlan parked behind it and turned to me.

"Do you have a plan?"

"No more than I did talking to Paddy McGrath. My plan is to tell them we know who they are, and why they're here, and get them to admit that they killed Glyn McTavish."

"That's a tall order. Why on earth would they tell you?"

I looked at him. "Because you're my five-dollar wrench."

Even as he chuckled, he said, "I'm no longer a violent creature."

"I know that, and you know that. But they don't know that."

"Just stick to your powers of persuasion, Quinn Callahan."

Hopefully they'd be good enough.

We walked up the drive to the large home that had been so dilapidated not very long ago and which Karen had worked her butt off and emptied her bank account to make charming and welcoming. She'd done a great job, I thought as we rang the bell.

Karen opened the door, looking slightly flustered.

"Is everything okay?" I asked her.

"Yes. Come in. You've caught us in a bit of an uproar."

We walked in. Over her shoulder she said, "I'm just getting the bills ready. One of my guests has suddenly decided to check out. Unexpectedly."

I didn't think it was the sudden departure that had her flustered, but the raised voices we could hear even from the doorway. It was the two Americans, and they were yelling insults so loudly I nearly covered my ears.

Lochlan and I exchanged a glance. It looked like we'd come just in the nick of time. And somehow I had to figure out how to stop them from heading home on a plane before they'd answered for their crimes, at least their recent crimes in Ireland.

The loud argument ceased the minute the two guys saw me and Lochlan. I'd overheard the squat one say to the tall one, "You gotta come with me," and the tall one reply, "No, Jimmy, I don't gotta do anything." From the heat surrounding them I suspected they'd been arguing for a while. Billy did his best to break into his usual toothy grin and act unconcerned.

"Why, Quinn Callahan. We have to stop meeting like this."

"Actually, I came to see you." I stared at him and then his partner. "Both of you."

The shorter one shook his head. "I gotta go. I'll be late for my flight."

I shook my head, trying to act as tough with him as I had

with Paddy McGrath. I wasn't doing that well, but having Lochlan at my back really added to my confidence. "You need to stay and listen to what I have to say."

Jimmy got big and scary-looking all of a sudden. "Oh yeah? Why's that?"

"Because I know all about Glen Morgan, and I can have the cops here long before you can get on a plane."

Jimmy's hand went automatically to his pocket and Lochlan said, cool as a cucumber, "I wouldn't."

The thug's eyes widened in shock. Lochlan looked so posh and urbane, but obviously Jimmy also saw his steel and menace because he dropped his hand. "I only got a minute."

"We'll see," I said.

"Quinn? What is all this about?" Karen asked, acting like my cat Cerridwen did in a lightning storm. Jumpy and kind of fizzy.

"I'll tell you later. Do you mind if we talk in the front room?"

"No. Help yourself." Then she sent an apologetic smile to Jimmy. "I'll have your bill ready when you come out."

I led the way and Lochlan brought up the rear, making sure the two men followed me. Once we were in the front room, Lochlan shut the door. It had the sound of finality, probably sounded like a prison door closing. Certainly the two men looked nervous. I felt the same. Lochlan was probably immune to gunfire, but I wasn't. And I didn't think I had a spell strong enough or fast enough to work against a gun fired at this close range.

However, I was determined to finish what I'd started. I said, "Why did you kill Glyn McTavish, or should I say Glen Morgan?"

"We didn't kill nobody," Jimmy said, looking angry.

"Come on, I know you're lying. I know all about Big Al."

Now Billy spoke up. "You work for him? Good luck to you, lady. He fired us."

Okay, that was a surprise I hadn't seen coming. "Why did Big Al fire you?"

"Said we didn't do the job right. Called us a pair of losers. Failures. Few other things I wouldn't say in front of a lady. He wasn't nice."

I doubted there was any employment standards branch that'd be interested in their complaints about unfair firing practices.

"You failed because you killed Glen Morgan." I was flying blind here, but following my instincts.

"Nah, why would we kill the guy? We needed him alive; we needed information."

"Would you shut your mouth," Jimmy said.

"Why should I? Big Al don't mean nothin' to me anymore. She wants to work for him? Good luck to her."

This was promising. Before I could even ask Billy the questions that were tumbling around in my mouth, he suddenly muttered in a sad tone, "I shoulda had the pork chop. I wanted the pork chop. I was gonna have the pork chop. And then you started on about the Irish stew. How you can't come to Ireland and not eat Irish stew. It's your fault I had the Irish stew. If I'd had the pork chop, we'd a done the job, got on the plane, and we'd be home now. Back where people talk English like normal, and they drive on the right side of the road, and their food don't make you sick."

"Now, that's not quite fair," Jimmy said. "The other stuff, I agree with you. But food at home can make you sick too.

Remember that time at Carmine Morelli's? We had the veal parmesan, and we was both sick for days."

"No, that wasn't Carmine Morelli's. That was Tito's place. That's where we had the veal parmesan. Morelli's was the bad meatballs. I couldn't get off the pot for three days."

"As much as I'm fascinated by the history of your gastrointestinal disasters, could we please talk about what happened at Glyn McTavish's place?"

Jimmy glared at me. "Nothin' happened. That's what I'm saying."

"You were seen going in. Next morning, Glyn McTavish was dead. You're telling me you had nothing to do with it?"

Billy said, "Yeah. That's what we're tellin' ya. Not saying we didn't plan to rough him up a little, 'cause we did. But before we could start, I had to puke so bad I barely made it to the john. And when I got back, my buddy here had his head out the backdoor. Can't intimidate nobody when you're retching your guts out."

I really wanted to laugh, but I couldn't. They just seemed so sorry for themselves that they hadn't been able to beat up the man because they had food poisoning. I held it together, though.

"So how did he end up dead, then?" Seemed like an excellent question under the circumstances.

"How do we know? But whoever killed him did us no favors. We probably still coulda rectified the situation, but the guy's dead. Can't get information out of a corpse."

That seemed indisputably true. I tried again. "Are you sure you didn't kill him because he knew who you were? And could turn you in to the police?"

They both laughed at that. "A man like Glen Morgan don't

want nothing to do with the police. They might find out who he really is. Or was."

"And who was he?" At least now we were getting somewhere. Also, I was beginning to believe that they hadn't killed the man.

"Glen Morgan worked for Big Al. He was his accountant," Billy said.

If Glen Morgan had stolen from a mob boss, he couldn't have been very bright. I was surprised he'd stayed alive as long as he had.

"He also got involved in this charity. Helping kids who don't got good homes, or somethin' like that," Jimmy added.

Billy said, "Big Al thought it was a good thing Glen was doin', so he didn't mind that Glen was doin' that on the side. But what none of us knew was that Glen was stealing money from the charity. Big Al, he'd do a lot of things, but not steal from little kids. Big Al had a tough start himself. He'd even given money to Glen's charity. When a couple mil went missing, he knew immediately who took it. But by then, Glen Morgan had disappeared like he'd never existed.

"Now Big Al holds grudges. He don't forget when somebody does him wrong, and he'd taken this personal, see? He puts the word out everywhere, but nobody sees Glen Morgan. Nobody hears a peep. Years go by. We all figured he was dead. Then all of a sudden, we get the call. Go to Ireland, Big Al says. He gives us Glen's address and everything."

"How did Big Al find him?"

Billy shook his head. "Beats me. Big Al didn't share anything else with us. Plays his cards close to his chest."

I locked my gaze on Jimmy. "When you were standing

outside the cottage that night, why did you ask Billy if he had the wrench?".

His expression hardly changed, but I could still see that I'd shocked him. "Did you have that place bugged?"

"As I said, you were seen." Just like Big Al, I could play my cards close to my chest. Need-to-know basis.

Billy and Jimmy were clearly accustomed to people who didn't tell them very much because they didn't question me further.

"Glen having crypto was an idea that Big Al's new accountant had. Didn't matter." Jimmy flexed his meaty hands. "Wherever Glen Morgan had that money hidden, we were going to find it."

"Did he tell you anything at all?"

"You think we'd still be in this bed and breakfast if he did?"

That was how I knew it was the truth. Of course they'd be gone if they'd found either the money or the way to get it.

After a short silence, Jimmy said, "If you're finished interrogating me, I got a plane to catch." And then he looked at Billy, who didn't seem to be in any hurry. "And you should come with. I bet we can get our jobs back."

Billy shook his head. "I kinda like it here. Think I might stay awhile. When's the last time either of us took a vacation?" Then he stared sadly at his partner. "You might think about staying, too. The atmosphere here might be healthier, if you know what I mean. Might live longer."

"Where are you planning to stay?" I asked him. The possibility of him squatting at Glyn McTavish's cottage crossed my mind, and if the Gardaí found him there, what a mess that would cause. Especially if he told them how much I'd known and not shared with them.

"Think I might stay here for a while."

I blinked, half stunned by this latest revelation. Billy was staying at Karen's B&B?

Billy nodded. "Time to look around me for the right opportunity."

"You're crazy," Jimmy said. "But I gotta go if I'm gonna make my plane." And he stomped toward the door and flung it open.

I followed Jimmy to where he grabbed his bag and his receipt from Karen. With a goofy expression on his face, Billy walked over to Karen as well. To my shock, she had a goofy expression going on, too.

"Dude," Billy's partner said, obviously unimpressed with this romantic turn of events. "Glen Morgan is dead. He never had his password written down. We looked everywhere. Face it. It died with him."

"Maybe," Billy said. "But it don't hurt to keep looking."

Jimmy made a motion like swatting a fly. "Bah. I give up on you. I give up." And then he glared at me. "And if you're finished with your questions, I gotta flight to catch."

And without waiting for an answer, he stalked to the door, opened it, and shut it behind him with a bang.

I LOOKED AT BILLY. "Are you sure about this?"

"Hey, how bad can it be? I got roots here. And I'm thinking it's not gonna be so good at home for a while. Or even forever. Big Al don't forgive people who don't get the job done right."

"You couldn't help getting sick," Karen said. Seemed like he'd told her everything if she knew who Big Al was, and that he'd failed in the job.

"Big Al won't see it that way." Then Billy turned to Lochlan. "So, you're the dude in the big castle, huh?"

"That's correct."

"You must have a few bucks."

Lochlan leveled him with a stare. "I do. I also run a multinational security firm. You mess with me, with Quinn, or any other person in Ballydehag, and I'll have you deported so fast you'll be touching down in New York before you realize you've left Ireland."

Billy raised his palms as though surrendering to a cop. "Hey, man, just making conversation."

"Good."

After that, Billy made an excuse to go upstairs. I looked at Lochlan.

"You didn't exactly welcome him to the neighborhood."

"I don't think we want him here."

"But you'll give him a chance, won't you?"

I had no idea why I suddenly felt so invested in Billy's future, except that Karen was my friend and I could see she quite liked him.

"My policy is everybody should get a second chance."

I thought his was a pretty good policy. Lochlan and I had both been given second chances, so I felt the same way.

"Can I meet you at your vehicle? I wouldn't mind chatting to Karen for a couple of minutes."

He said that was fine and left. I knew if I needed him, all I had to do was call his name, and he'd return immediately.

Karen was hovering by the antique desk where she did the checking in and checking out. She looked half embarrassed and half thrilled.

I said to her, "You and Billy?"

Now she looked a little bit more of both those things. "I know, Quinn. Doesn't make much sense. But he's nice when you get to know him."

I said as gently as I could, "You do know that he's a paid thug, right? Probably connected with the mafia in New York?"

"Yes, I know. He told me all about it."

"And you don't mind?"

"I thought it was kind of exciting, to be honest. He swears he's never killed anybody. And, now he's met me, he says he really wants to change his ways."

I tried not to be too cynical, but that sounded like a total line to me. Maybe he was sincere. Who was I to say?

"But what's he going to do if he stays?" No doubt there were gangs of unpleasant people around, but did we really want Billy getting himself connected to the Irish mafia?

"He's got some savings. And he also has a few ideas," she added.

"He's not going to try to buy Glyn McTavish's old cottage, is he?"

"It's a great property in a nice area. Yeah, he's thinking about it. He even found out who owns it." She shot me a 'you'll never guess' look.

I raised my eyebrows, knowing she was dying to spill.

"Billy had a really difficult time discovering who the

cottage's owners were because Glyn McTavish paid cash for his rent, and Sean didn't declare it."

"Sean? As in Higgins, not O'Grady?"

Karen nodded. Of course, Sean and Rosie Higgins owned the cottage. Why was I not surprised?

"I think they'll sell it to Billy now someone's died there," she said.

"But it's a crime scene. He can't exactly move in right away."

Now she blushed and looked at the desktop as though it was fascinating. "He's going to stay with me for a while. I won't charge him much. He can help me out."

If I thought that hiring an American mafia thug to help out in a charming Irish bed and breakfast was not the smartest idea I'd ever heard, I kept that opinion to myself. Karen was a grownup. Presumably, she knew what she was doing.

I'd keep an eye on Billy, though. And knowing Lochlan, I wouldn't even have to ask him. He'd be keeping an eye on Billy, too.

"What can Billy do in your bed and breakfast?" I had a feeling his cooking skills weren't too hot.

"He can help me with the bags. You'd be surprised what heavy luggage some people turn up at a B&B with. And my back isn't very strong. I can't be hauling cases up the stairs all day long."

Okay, I could picture Billy being pretty good as a porter. He was certainly muscular.

"So, that'll take about ten minutes a day. What else is he going to do?" I did not want her being taken advantage of.

"He says he's got a huge family in New York. He knows

loads of people who might like to come to a pretty little village in Ireland for a vacation."

Oh, good, Billy's 'family' was just who I didn't think we wanted to welcome here. Hopefully, he'd quickly realize what a terrible idea that was. Maybe I could drop the hint that he'd be far better to keep a low profile for a while. Preferably a long while.

CHAPTER 16

The next day, I was walking down the high street for my daily coffee when I caught sight of Beatrice standing outside Giles Murray's photographic studio. I hadn't heard she'd returned from visiting her mother, but it seemed she had. Presumably she and Giles were still together. As I walked past her, I said, "Hello, Beatrice, welcome back."

She jumped and swung around to me, her eyes wide.

I hadn't exactly bellowed in her ear, so her reaction startled me as much as I'd frightened her. "I'm so sorry. I didn't mean to scare you."

She put a hand to her chest. "It wasn't your fault. I'm a little jumpy today. I was miles away."

Giles came out then and took her hand. "My poor love," he said to her before he turned to me. "Beatrice's still looking at bit peaky, isn't she? Truth is, she hasn't been very well. She went to see her mother for a few days to be looked after properly. Apparently, Mummy can do a better job than me." He laughed as though we'd both argue that wasn't true.

She did look peaky, too.

I said to her, "Did you eat the stew at Sean O'Grady's pub the other night?" I realized now that that was the last time I'd seen her.

Giles patted her hand. "Yes. Yes, she did. Didn't want to make any more trouble, so she didn't say anything. She's fine now. Aren't you, love?"

"Yes," she said in her soft voice. "I'm fine now."

I continued on my way, and the pair of them disappeared into the photographic shop. I got my coffee and found that I was so distracted I said yes to a go-cup when I'd intended to sit and stay. They weren't so big on the go-cups in Ballydehag. I sometimes thought they only stocked them for me.

Once I had my go-cup, I felt too foolish to sit down and drink it at one of the tables, so I headed out again. I strolled back to The Blarney Tome and, peeking in the window, could see that Dierdre wasn't overrun with customers, so on instinct I kept going. I walked into Sean O'Grady's pub. Instead of the usual scent of spilled beer, the place smelled like disinfectant. Poor Sean, he wasn't taking any chances.

I found him in the kitchen scrubbing down the counters. He wore bright blue, industrial rubber gloves. He looked surprised to see me.

"Quinn. We won't be serving lunch for another forty-five minutes."

"I know. I just had a question for you. Do you remember what Beatrice had for dinner on the Friday night when some got sick from the Irish stew?"

He looked thoroughly irritated by my question, and I couldn't really blame him. "Quinn, I'm really trying to put this behind me. What on earth do you want to know that for?" Before I could explain, he went on a rant. "I don't know what more I can do. My hands are raw from scrubbing. I chucked every bit of food, condiment, spice, hundreds of euros worth. Probably thousands. I'm not even sure my business will survive. And now you want to know what some random customer had to eat on a night I'd rather forget?"

"I do understand. Really, I do. But I'm trying to figure out the truth." For a moment, I thought for sure he was going to throw me out, me and my nosy questions.

He did not look pleased, but he stomped over to the computer where he kept his bookings, yanked off his rubber gloves with a flourish, and slapped them down on the counter. They made a sound like a whip. I was clearly being punished. Still, he did as I asked.

With great sighs and huffs of frustration, he banged keys and then said, "For your information, Ms. Callahan, Beatrice had fish and chips on the Friday in question." Then he turned to me. "Will there be anything else? Do you want to know what Father O'Flanagan had for lunch last week Tuesday? How many whiskeys Danny might have consumed a fortnight ago? Don't hesitate to ask. I'm at your service." His sarcasm was as strong as the smell of bleach. Maybe stronger.

I backed away slowly. "I'm really sorry to trouble you. I'll let you get back to your work."

He put his rubber gloves back on with the finesse of a surgeon about to replace a heart and then said, "Appreciate it."

I left the kitchen with my suspicion confirmed, but no closer to the truth. Why on earth would Giles have lied about Beatrice having food poisoning? No one who'd eaten anything other than the Irish stew had become ill. And yet, she had looked pale. Was there something else going on? Was she ill with something else? Had they, in fact, broken up? Maybe he'd begged her to return, and she was trying to find the courage to leave him. I had no idea. As usual, by poking around I'd only uncovered a few more questions to answer and no answers to the questions I had.

Still, every bit of the truth seemed like one tiny piece of a jigsaw puzzle. The trouble with this puzzle was it was one of those that had all blue sky and blue ocean, and they were the most devious ones of all.

As I walked from the pub to my bookshop, I couldn't help thinking about Dorian Gray. Appearances can be deceiving. No book ever made that clearer. Something was going on that appeared fine on the outside but was filled with ugliness on the inside.

That had already played out in Glyn McTavish living here as a supposedly harmless recluse, while his hidden portrait was all that money he'd stolen from a children's charity. How that must have burned away at him. He'd quickly realized he couldn't spend it without being found by people who would happily kill him for his betrayal. He couldn't enjoy his wealth in any way. And, as an accountant, I wonder if it pierced his soul every time he got another whack-load of interest and that hidden fortune increased even more, as impossible for him to spend as it would be if he'd left it where it belonged.

And now, rather like that portrait, the fortune might remain hidden for a very long time. Perhaps forever. If only I could figure out the key, we could give the money back. But how?

I had a very bad feeling that the secret had died with Glyn McTavish.

Outside the bookshop, I paused to check my phone for

messages, then posted a quote from Oscar Wilde on The Blarney Tome's Instagram account. I put that together with the most flattering picture of Oscar Wilde that I could find online. I was so busy buttering up that touchy vampire he'd slip through my hands if I tried to touch him.

Instagram. Of course.

Then, instead of going into The Blarney Tome, I veered across the street and up to Giles Murray's photographic studio. I walked in to find Beatrice hard at work typing something on the computer and Giles looking over some contact sheets. He still did business in portrait photography. He glanced up when I came in.

"Quinn. Twice in one day. How can I help you?"

I said, "I come with good news. Lochlan's happy for you to launch your book at the castle."

His face was suddenly suffused with smiles. He leapt out of his seat, threw his arms around me, and gave me a big hug. "Thank you, my dear. I knew you'd do it. If I'd gone up to the castle and asked for a book launch, I'd have been sent on my way with a boot up my backside, but send a lovely thing like you and I knew he'd be putty in your hands."

The effusive bonhomie was a bit much, but I was pleased he was so happy. "Lochlan suggests that you come up to the castle tomorrow night. We need to discuss the details. Decide what goes where, how many people are on your guest list, what kind of catering you want. You know, figure out the logistics."

He nodded eagerly. "That'd be grand. And, you remember those lovely, big posters you had for Bartholomew Branson's launch. Of course, being a photographer, I can commission some lovely, full-length photographic posters. Very tasteful. This book showcases some of my best work."

I tried to sound as excited as he did. "That's fantastic. I think it's going to be a really grand event. I could run book sales for you, if you'd like."

Here he laughed. "Lochlan's being so enthusiastic, perhaps he'll allow me to photograph himself and his castle for volume two of *Ireland through my Lens*."

I gave a hearty chuckle of my own. He was already thinking about volume two? "You never know." I glanced at Beatrice. "So, we'll see you both at seven tomorrow?"

"Absolutely. Wouldn't miss it." Giles answered for her as usual.

As I left the photographic studio, I only had one thing left to do before I went back to my own shop. I needed to let Lochlan know that he'd just agreed to host another book launch.

He was not going to be thrilled.

FRIDAY NIGHT CAME and with it, a fearful sense that I might be about to make a huge fool of myself. I consoled myself that it wouldn't be the first time and certainly not the last. Still, I'd really prefer not to humiliate myself in front of people whose opinion not only mattered to me, but in some cases they could put me in jail. However, a strong sense that this very blurry picture was starting to come into focus made me bold enough to continue with my plan.

Such as it was.

When I arrived at the castle, I found that Lochlan at least

had taken me seriously. He'd prepared everything as I'd asked him to.

Bartholomew Branson was there, not looking very pleased with himself. I suspected his nose was put out of joint that we were having yet another book launch so soon after his. Also, I was almost certain he was measuring the dimensions of the posters that Giles had promised to provide, making sure that they weren't larger than his had been.

Dierdre was fluttering around doing I really didn't know what, and then Oscar Wilde strolled in, resplendent in purple and yellow with a polka dot scarf around his neck and a hat perched rakishly on his head. He was the epitome of the picturesque.

"No book launch for me, I see," he said, sounding bored, but I heard the quiver of irritation in his tone, too.

We'd featured his book in the book club, what more did he want? "Oscar," I said, walking over to him, "you saw what happened when we tried to launch a new Bartholomew Branson. Don't tell me there's a new Oscar Wilde?"

He looked down his nose at me. "Obviously not. I'm not some workaday hack, pounding out words with no thought to their quality. Everything I had to say, I said in my life. And no one has ever reflected society in a more accurate glass."

Bartholomew Branson snorted. "If by glass you mean mirror, you're never going to reflect anything in a glass ever again. Face it, buddy, you're dead."

Oscar sneered at him. "But my brilliance and talent will outlive your turgid prose, and we both know it."

We all knew it, so there was general silence. Then Bartholomew stomped off to complain to Dierdre, who led him out of the gallery. Bless her, she was such a good listener.

As we had other guests arriving, I suggested that Oscar might also like to make himself scarce.

He glanced at the advanced copy I was holding and shook his head. "So that's his precious art. All art is quite useless."

So was arguing with the flamboyant vampire when he was in one of his moods. However, with a tap of his ebony walking stick and a swish of his velvet cloak, he turned and headed out of the gallery. He was dressed for the outdoors, but I suspected that was another pose. He wouldn't leave before it was full dark and most of Ballydehag was asleep, and that was hours away yet. I was certain he and some of the other vampires would be watching from the secret gallery that overlooked this large space.

Sean O'Grady arrived soon after to talk through the catering menu for Giles Murray's book launch.

"You'll be serving traditional Irish food, I imagine, to go with the theme of this book," Lochlan said.

"I will." Though he went a little red in the face and blustered, "But if you don't mind, Mr. Balfour, I won't be serving my Irish stew."

And who could blame him? I don't think any of us would have eaten it, anyway. He wasn't as effusively friendly to me as he normally was, until Lochlan told him it was my idea that he should do the catering. I understood he was still annoyed with me about my barging into his kitchen and interrogating him, but hopefully it was all going to be for a good cause.

Lochlan came over to me. "I do hope you know what you're doing, Quinn," he said.

I had really counted on his support, and even the slight wobble was worrying. "I hope so, too."

The truth was I really had no idea, but some theories

have to be acted out to be proven. I suspected this was one of those. If it didn't work, I'd have years to live down my foolishness.

We were interrupted when Giles Murray and Beatrice came in holding hands. She was looking better, not so pale, but there was still an anxious look in her eyes as she glanced around the huge hall as though she'd never been there before, when I'd seen her there on more than one occasion. Giles came forward full of smiles and good humor. He went straight up to Lochlan and held out his hand.

As they shook he said, "I'm very pleased that you've decided to host this book launch, Lochlan. You're doing a fine thing, not only for me, but for Ballydehag and Ireland itself."

That might be a bit grandiose, but Lochlan took it in good part, merely saying, "I believe in keeping a record of the old ways." And he remembered old ways that went a lot farther back than Giles could even imagine. It crossed my mind that if he were to ever sit down and write a book, it would be riveting. I watched that cool, aristocratic face and knew he'd never do such a thing. Whatever his story, whatever his past, it was locked away behind that calm façade.

There was a moment, an awkward pause, when Giles glanced around as though expecting to be entertained. I still had a couple more actors yet to arrive in this play I was putting on, though Giles and Beatrice didn't know it.

I came forward and said, "I'm so excited that we can do this. I was wondering about the measurements for the posters."

"What do you think about putting the big posters here? And here?" I asked, pointing to enormous wall spaces that weren't already covered with tapestry.

He nodded, enthusiastic. He pulled out his phone and showed me the mock-ups he'd already made for the posters. I had to say, they looked great.

He said, "I've gone black and white, of course, in keeping with the aesthetics of the castle. Also, black and white suggests the past and some of these faces clearly harken back to days gone by."

I nodded, though I had to think that really, a face that was living today was contemporary, even if they still looked like their ancestors who'd been hoeing potatoes a hundred years ago. But I didn't say anything. Giles had his vision, and it wasn't up to me, a mere bookseller, to disturb it. I sold the books; I didn't write them.

I was about to take him over to talk to Sean O'Grady about food when, fortunately, there was a slight commotion and the two people I'd been hoping would arrive did.

Giles jerked to a stop and his eyebrows rose. "You called in the Gardaí? Isn't that overkill?"

"It's for security," I explained. "If you remember, there was a little trouble at our last book launch." And a *little* was putting it mildly. "Lochlan felt that if we had a police presence here, providing security, that there wouldn't be any trouble."

I didn't know whether Giles had bought it or not, but at that moment Lochlan came over and said, "I hope you don't mind, Giles, but having the Gardaí on hand was a condition of me agreeing to do this book launch."

His hesitation was over. "Of course, of course, I perfectly understand." He gave a dry chuckle. "Though I hope a book of portraits of locals won't cause as much kerfuffle as an American thriller."

We all chuckled.

And I said, "You never know."

Sergeant Kelly didn't look any more happy to be here than Giles Murray looked to have him. I knew I didn't have a whole lot of time. It was Friday evening, after all, and even detectives must have some kind of social life. At least, I hoped they did.

This, then, was the critical moment.

Lochlan said to Giles, "Why don't you come with me, and we'll discuss the arrangements with the detectives. I want to make sure you're happy with everything I've got planned." He gave his charming smile. "I do work in security, after all. You'll have to forgive me if I'm a little overcautious."

"Not at all, not at all. I perfectly understand. And, as I said, I'm only grateful for your assistance in this book launch. I'm hoping to get my editor and a few of the publicity people out. It's an excellent opportunity for them to see the Ireland I've portrayed. I've an idea that there might be a TV series in this, too."

Lochlan nodded and began to lead him away. Giles's hand was still clutched in Beatrice's, and I moved smoothly between them and separated their hands.

"If you don't mind, Giles, I'm going to borrow Beatrice for a minute. I need her help with costumes."

CHAPTER 17

Both Beatrice and Giles gaped at me in a shocked way. And who could blame them? I had sprung this on them.

"Costumes?" Giles asked, not sounding best pleased.

I put on my gushiest voice. And when I try, I can gush with the best of them. "Yes, isn't it just the best idea? I thought we'd all dress up in traditional Irish garb. It's going to be so great, isn't it?"

Now there was a moment when Giles clearly wanted to tell me it was the stupidest idea he'd ever heard of. And I didn't disagree. But I could see him doing the mental calculations. I was the one who'd talked Lochlan into having this shindig. If he shut me down about costumes, might he lose my goodwill?

I played on that as hard as I could. I said, "It was all my idea. I really had to talk Lochlan into it. I'm super excited about this. I'm sure we can get some local media too."

Over Lochlan's dead body, if it wasn't dead already.

Giles put on a seriously fake happy face and said, "Well,

I'm sure if you think it's a good idea, Quinn, and especially if it gets us some extra publicity, I'm willing to go along with it."

"That's great," I said enthusiastically. "Beatrice, I've got the prettiest dress I want you to wear. Come with me."

I didn't give her a chance to think about it. I grabbed the hand that hadn't recently been holding Giles's and dragged her along with me. We left the main hall, and I took her up a flight of stairs to a bedroom that had been prepared. Like the other rooms that I tended to use, Lochlan made sure there was a heating source. It was warm and the wine and glasses were out waiting.

I said, "Would you like some wine?"

She was so nervous she didn't seem to know what she wanted. She glanced around as though Giles might appear at her side to tell her what to do like he usually did. But he wasn't there.

"Oh. I'm not..."

I made up her mind for her. I poured out a glass of wine. And then I poured one for myself. "They'll be ages talking about security. We can have some girl time. I don't have many female friends in this village. It's nice to be able to talk to another woman."

She nodded like a scared rabbit. If scared rabbits nodded. "Yes. I know what you mean."

I said, "It must be hard for you, too. You don't seem to have a lot of friends in this village outside of Giles."

"We do everything together."

That was exactly what I was hoping.

She sipped her wine, then put it down so the glass clicked on the table. She glanced around. "What kind of costume did you have in mind? I'm not sure I really want to play dress-up."

"It will be fun," I said again. I went to the wardrobe and showed her three dresses that I'd had the vampires unearth from their various trunks.

That was one thing about vampires. They tended to have clothes that went back for centuries. It was really important to me that I give Beatrice a reason to stay and, hopefully, relax. Maybe choosing clothes would keep her occupied enough so that I'd be able to really talk to her. In spite of herself, she was drawn to the dresses. She pulled out a simple corseted Victorian frock with blue fabric stitched with little flowers.

"Oh, this is pretty," she said, holding the dress against her.

"I'm glad you think so. I thought the color would enhance your eyes. Do you want to try it on?"

She looked around vaguely. I pointed to the screen that we'd already put in place. It was like something you'd find in an old stage star's dressing room.

She went behind the screen, and I heard the rustling of clothing coming off and more rustling as the new clothing went on. I made sure there was a mirror back there too so she could catch her reflection before she came out to see me. And believe me, finding a mirror in a castle filled with vampires had not been easy. I'd found one tucked away in the back of a cupboard in a disused bedroom.

Behind the screen, she was silent long enough that I was pretty sure she was admiring her own reflection. And then she came out looking really pleased. And she did look gorgeous.

I said, "Giles is going to fall over himself when he sees you in that dress. He should take your portrait. You've been a big part of this project, haven't you?"

Her nervous hands fluttered over the silk. "Oh, not really. I just help him."

"You're more than a helper. He says you're his muse."

She laughed softly. "He flatters me."

I said, changing my tone and the atmosphere immediately, "You didn't eat the Irish stew the night people got sick, though, did you?"

The soft blush in her cheeks died along with the pleased expression in her eyes. "What do you mean?"

Not an answer. "Beatrice, I checked. You had the fish and chips that night. Why did you lie to me? Or why did you let Giles lie to me?"

She looked as though she might make a run for it, but I was standing between her and the door. "I don't know. Anyone can make a mistake. I suppose he thought I had the Irish stew, and I couldn't remember. I mean, who remembers what they ate a week ago?"

"Anyone who ate something that made them sick tends to remember it." I was playing both good cop and bad cop here, and I felt sorry that I was being so hard on her. But it was important. In the way that the truth was important.

"I think Giles didn't want to be honest about the reason I left." She said it haltingly.

"What do you mean? Why not?"

Her eyes filled with tears. "Because I was thinking of leaving him."

Crap. This had been my greatest fear, that I'd penned a whole story and got the plot wrong. "I'm sorry to hear that. What made you come back?"

"He begged me," she said. "He said he can't live without me. And I'm not sure who I am without him."

I had the sudden image of Sybil Vane in *The Picture of Dorian Gray*. A woman who was gifted and brilliant in the eyes of her admirer until her love for him made her dull in his eyes. Had that happened to Beatrice?

I had to press on. "There's more to it than that, isn't there? Beatrice, I know what you did."

Big, fat lie. I didn't have a clue what she'd done, but I had a few suspicions. She went deathly white and sat down on the nearest chair. A deep, leather club chair that seemed to engulf her like an enormous fist.

"I didn't. I haven't. I don't know what you're talking about."

I pushed on. "Yes, you do. You were there that night. You were in Glyn McTavish's cottage the night he died."

She shook her head back and forth so hard her whole body twisted. "No. No. I wasn't. I didn't. I have to go downstairs."

She stood up, and I placed myself in front of her. "You are going to feel so much better when you tell someone about this. I can see it's eating away at you. Lies are like poison. They eat away at you. Beatrice," I said in my most commanding voice. "Why did you kill Glyn McTavish?"

She pushed past me, and she was stronger than she looked. "No. I didn't. I'm going. You can't keep me here." And with all the drama of a soap opera star, she threw open the door and ran down the hall.

I heard her feet pounding down the stairs into the big room. I followed more slowly.

When I got to the bottom of the stairs, she had thrown herself into Giles's arms. "Take me home. I want to go home. I don't like it here."

He looked down at her. "Darling, calm down. You're hysterical." There was command in his voice.

She was crying, sobbing now, with her head buried in his chest. The two Gardaí officers looked at me. I crossed to take my place in the middle of the room. I could have been a soap opera star too.

"You'd be upset too, Giles, if someone accused you of murder." I let those words hang.

He wrapped his arms more tightly around Beatrice. "Murder? What on earth are you talking about?"

"You were there too, Giles. At Glyn McTavish's cottage the night he died. You know you were. Beatrice never ate the stew that night. That wasn't why she left Ballydehag the day Glyn McTavish's body was discovered. That's not why she's looked pale and frightened ever since she returned. That's her guilty conscience. I told her she'll feel a lot better if she admits her crime."

He looked absolutely furious. "What nonsense is this? My Beatrice couldn't hurt a fly. She's the gentlest soul alive."

"Then why did you lie about her eating that stew? Why did she leave?"

"I won't stand here and see my poor girl insulted like this. I'm afraid we're leaving."

But the two Gardaí officers had quietly moved and were standing in front of the exit.

"I'd be obliged if you'd answer the question, sir," Detective Inspector Walsh said in a calm, conversational tone.

"But this is an outrage. Why on earth would Beatrice kill Glyn McTavish?"

"I've been wondering that myself," I said. "And I have a theory."

He gave a spurt of annoyed laughter. "Forgive me if I'm not interested in your ridiculous theories. I've got a book to launch and my sweet Beatrice to calm down." He put his arm around her and led her, still weeping, toward the two officers.

As much as every man hates a weeping female, I really hoped they would stand their ground. And they did.

"Very sorry for the young lady, sir, but we have reason to believe you were in the cottage that night."

"This is an outrage," he said again. He was really in love with that phrase.

"Nevertheless, sir, just to help us with our enquiries. We could do it down at the station if you prefer."

He turned to me, rigid and furious. "Was this a trick? Was this whole thing a trick? Are you not planning to launch my book after all?"

"Right now, I'm more worried about a murderer going free, than your book launch."

He glanced around, but Lochlan had also moved forward a couple of steps. Sean O'Grady, who had quite an interest in the outcome of this discussion, had also moved. He came out from behind his table and stood with his arms crossed, staring at the photographer. It was only the two police officers who hadn't moved.

"This is ridiculous. Why would you dream up such a tale? Just tell me why."

"I'll tell you a story. A story complete with photographs," I said. "You like stories that go with pictures, don't you, Giles?"

"I really don't have time for your stupid puzzles and games."

"Fair enough. I'll just give it to you straight. Here's what happened. I've been thinking about how you've tried to get all the interesting characters in the neighborhood in your book." I picked up his advanced copy and held it as though I were a teacher in front of an eager class. I turned the pages and described the pictures. "Here's Danny, holding up the bar at the pub. Here's Father O'Flanagan, tending his roses in front of the old church. Here's a woman I don't know gardening. A farmer digging up potatoes. You've gone far and wide looking for the picturesque. And yet, Glyn McTavish—a crusty, old hermit living in an abandoned stone cottage—could not be more picturesque. But where is his picture?"

He huffed with annoyance. "Where is Lochlan Balfour's picture? Not everyone wanted their picture taken, Quinn. I hope I respect their choices."

"But I don't think you did. I don't think you respected Glyn McTavish's choices at all. I think you took his picture."

He puffed up like a rooster about to crow. "And do you see his picture in that book, Ms. Callahan?" he said with awful sarcasm.

"No. I do not. But you know where I found it? On your Instagram feed."

"But I deleted it."

CHAPTER 18

In the terrible silence that followed, Giles Murray scrambled to find words. "I mean, I mean I deleted the page in the book that I had intended for Glyn McTavish. You're right, he was a crusty old recluse who would have made a wonderful portrait for the book. But he refused, and that's all there is to it."

I shook my head. "You took his photograph on the sly, without his permission. Then you put it on the Instagram account you've been boasting about. You deleted the post after he died. But not before an awful lot of people had seen it."

"You can't prove that."

"Actually, I can." And I'd never been so happy to have a friend as tech savvy as Lochlan Balfour.

Through some kind of hacker means known only to himself, he had been able to get into Giles Murray's account and find his history, including deleted posts. At my nod, he pressed a button and up slid a screen cleverly hidden in a side table. He hit another button and an Instagram post—

clearly from Giles Murray's account—displayed on the screen. There was no mistaking the man sitting on a chair on the porch of that ramshackle cottage, reading.

I said, "Not only did you post that picture to your Instagram account, but you got nearly two thousand likes."

"And if I did? That doesn't prove anything. So I took a picture of a man and put it on Instagram. I took it down, didn't I?"

"Yes. But not until he was dead. You deleted that post the day after Glyn died. The same day Beatrice left town."

Giles turned to DI Walsh. "I'd like to press charges against Quinn Callahan for hacking into my personal Instagram account. That must be a crime. It's an absolute outrage and invasion of my privacy."

I appreciated his bluster, but I suspected solving a murder was more important than his hacked account.

DI Walsh obviously agreed. "I'd like to get this issue of the murder explained away first, sir, if you don't mind."

"There's nothing to say. Beatrice didn't kill the man. Why would she?"

Once more, I had the answer. "You went there that night to try to convince him one last time to let you put his picture in your book. And to flatter him, you showed him that Instagram post, didn't you? So he could see how many likes it had."

Beatrice sobbed louder. It wasn't an answer, but it was something.

So, I continued. "I can see it as though it was a movie. You took Beatrice along, because you take her everywhere, and you knocked on the door. Knowing Glyn McTavish, he probably didn't answer. Somehow you got him to open the door and let you in. And then you tried to sweet-talk him into being in your book. You pulled out your phone, and you showed him that post. I've seen you do it a hundred times. And I've seen the way people are flattered when they discover how many likes there are of a picture of themselves. But Glyn McTavish didn't respond the way most of your portrait subjects have, did he?"

"Oh, I can't bear it," Beatrice said and put her hands over her ears.

Giles said, "Can't you stop this? Look how you're upsetting her."

"You can stop it any time. Tell us what happened."

"I won't. You're making up a ridiculous story. You have no evidence."

He was obviously right. The only weapon I had right now was Beatrice. And as bad as I felt, I was pushing as hard as I could. Maybe Giles Murray wouldn't crack, but I was pretty sure Beatrice was very close to it. I dug my fingernails into my palms because I hated causing her pain, and it was physically hurting me to do so.

I continued with my story. And so far, that was all it was. "Glyn McTavish flew into a rage. Because what you didn't know, but Glyn McTavish did, was that you had disclosed his whereabouts to the people he'd been hiding from for years. He attacked you. And Beatrice, not knowing what else to do, grabbed a fire poker and struck him over the back of the head."

"No," Beatrice screamed.

Tears were streaming down her face, and she was heaving in breaths, which—while wearing that corseted gown—was going to make her faint.

I glared at Giles. "How can you put her through this? Tell us the truth."

When he glanced at Beatrice, in that moment, I thought he really did love her. He brought a hand to his forehead.

"It wasn't Beatrice who killed him. It was me." He let out a huge sigh, and his shoulders slumped forward in defeat. "You're right, Quinn. Exactly right up until the point where Glyn McTavish went into the rage. He was already in a rage when we got there. Someone had told him about my Instagram post, and he was ranting, saying terrible things to us. As I've told you, Beatrice would never hurt anyone. She shrank into a corner, screaming. We fought. It was me who grabbed the fire poker. Me who struck him down. I didn't mean to kill him." He looked at the Gardaí with appeal. "It was clearly self-defense."

"That's for your lawyer to argue, sir."

Giles threw his hands in the air. "I didn't know what to do."

"You should have called us, sir. That is the correct procedure."

"I know I should have. But I panicked. I panicked, all right? I had no way to prove it was self-defense. No one had seen us. Beatrice was in hysterics. I knew I had to get her out of there. But I didn't want to be embroiled in a sordid investigation, not with my book coming out. He was an old man, a recluse. Who would even miss him?"

"So you moved the body," I said.

He'd only be confirming what the police investigation had uncovered.

He nodded. "I could see he'd been in bed eating his stew before we interrupted him." He looked at the woman sobbing in his arms. "And this is the part I feel the most terrible about. I made my poor angel help me move him. We dragged him into his bedroom and laid him out, trying to make it look as though he'd tripped getting out of bed and fallen and hit his head. Which could have happened. It could happen to anyone."

~

As Giles Murray's words echoed off the stone walls, I felt my tension dissipate in a whoosh. I had done it. My gamble had paid off. Pushing poor Beatrice practically into a breakdown had been worth the pain. For me at least. For Glyn McTavish too.

"But there's more," I said. "Glyn McTavish was packing up, wasn't he? He'd planned to leave that cottage before his enemies found him."

Giles Murray turned to stare at me. "How could you possibly know that? We put everything back."

"You left one of the packing boxes on the floor beside the bookcase. And you put his books back in the wrong order."

"Oh, come on. Are you psychic or something?"

Or something. But in this case I hadn't needed any stronger powers than a good pair of eyes and a brain. "I was the one who discovered his body, remember? I looked at his library while we were waiting for the Gardaí to arrive. I noticed at the time that there was no rhyme or reason to the way the books were arranged. And yet everything else in Glyn McTavish's cottage was so orderly, it didn't make sense. You unpacked his books, didn't you? You shoved them back on the shelves."

He must know that compared to killing a man, reshelving a few books wasn't going to make much difference to his punishment. He nodded.

"Was anything else packed?"

"No. Just the books. He hadn't started on the rest of the cottage yet."

In the heavy silence that followed, we all looked to DI Walsh.

He nodded to Sergeant Kelly, who finally strode toward Giles and the weeping Beatrice and said, "You'll need to come down to the station with us. Where we'll ask you to repeat what you've just told us."

Giles said, "Not Beatrice, surely? I've just explained to you. She had nothing to do with this."

"We'll need both of you, sir."

Before Giles and Beatrice—in company with the two detectives—had reached the doorway, I said, "You didn't just move the body, did you?"

Once more I found myself the center of attention.

"What else did you do?" I asked, focusing on Giles.

He rubbed his cheeks with his palms. "What does it matter?"

I said, "Tell me about the books."

Detective Inspector Walsh said, "Do you mean the books in Glyn McTavish's cottage?"

I nodded, keeping my gaze on Giles. He must know it wouldn't make any difference at this point. He seemed to kind of slump into himself.

"When we arrived, McTavish was obviously preparing to leave. He had most of his books in boxes. I thought it would look more like he died a natural death if he wasn't in the middle of packing up his house. So, after we'd put him in the bedroom, Beatrice and I put the books back on the bookshelf. Beatrice was in a state, so I did most of it. She was beside herself to get out of there, so I just shoved the books back any way I could."

"And what did you do with the boxes?"

He looked at me as though he were considering whether I might be a witch. The strange thing was I wasn't using any magic here. This was pure deductive power. I was finding my sleuthing powers got better the more I used them. Like practicing my craft.

"How do you know about the boxes?"

"Because you left one behind. I figured there had to be more."

He nodded. "I put them in the back of my car and disposed of them. They were just ordinary grocery boxes. Nothing special."

I nodded. I'd known that. Except they'd been numbered.

DI Walsh was looking at me with a considering expression on his face. He must wonder as much as Giles did why I was so interested in those books. I didn't like lying to the authorities, so once again I stayed as close to the truth as I could. Or, in this case, gave a partial truth.

I said, "I'm a bookseller, remember? I noticed that Glyn McTavish had some very fine volumes on his shelves. I just wondered why they were so disordered, when he seemed to be such an orderly man."

Giles shook his head. "I wasn't thinking clearly, obviously. Not in the state of mind to follow the Dewey Decimal System. Beatrice was having hysterics. I had a dead man in the next room. I wasn't too worried about shelving books in alphabetical order."

"I understand." And I was glad he'd put together that one very annoying puzzle piece that had been missing.

~

WE WAITED until they were gone, then Lochlan said, "The books. Of course."

I was pleased he'd followed the same line of thought I had.

Sean O'Grady spoke up then. "But I don't understand. What did my stew have to do with anything?" He looked both puzzled and furious. "I had to close my pub, clean the restaurant like it's never been cleaned in its life, put up with a nasty review on my website that I don't know how to take down, and all for nothing?"

Lochlan said, "I'll assign a technician to your website. I'm sure, under the circumstances, we can have that taken down."

"Yes, but me reputation in town is in tatters. I don't even understand what happened. First Glyn McTavish is poisoned by the stew, then he wasn't. He died of natural causes, then he didn't. What is going on here?"

They were excellent points. I couldn't tell him everything, because I didn't think Sean O'Grady was going to buy my story about leprechauns. And besides, I could never prove what I was fairly certain had happened. I stuck as close to the truth as I could in a way that a one hundred percent mortal human would understand.

"I've been doing some research on that, Sean. Here's what

I think happened. You made your beautiful Irish stew as you always do. And you put bay leaves in it. Am I right?"

"Of course. I always put bay leaves in the Irish stew. What of it?"

"Well, I'm sure you're aware that the Cherry Laurel has a very similar leaf, and I think some of those accidentally got mixed in with your regular stash of bay leaves. And after you'd served a few bowls, you came in and thought another bay leaf or two were needed to add a little extra flavor." I was flying by the seat of my pants here.

He looked puzzled. "Why would I add more bay leaves?"

This was a sticking point in my story. "I don't know, but you must have done. It's the only thing that makes sense. Because the first people that ate your stew were fine and the ones who ate it later got sick."

In fact, what I was now fairly sure had happened was that Mr. Paddy McGrath had got his wife to sneak into the kitchen at some point. I didn't think leprechauns had the ability to make themselves invisible, but they were cunning creatures, as I'd already discovered. She must have waited until everyone's back was turned, sneaked in and stuck some of the poisonous bay leave look-alikes into the stew, not planning to kill anyone, which she obviously hadn't. But they put the fake bay leaves into the stew to make the thugs from New York sick enough that they wouldn't be able to pressure the secret password out of Glyn McTavish. They needed time to find that treasure for themselves.

Sean O'Grady looked extremely confused. I could tell he was thinking back to that night, a night he must have run over and over in his head by now. He'd wracked his brain so often, been questioned about it so often, that I suspected it was all a bit of a blur. I didn't even need to use my magic to get him sufficiently confused that he said, "I suppose it's possible."

Lochlan spoke up now. "I think it's best we just put the whole fiasco behind us. There's an Irish heritage fund whose board I sit on. I may be able to get you compensated for what you've been through. Enough that your business won't suffer."

I suspected there was no such foundation, and that Lochlan would take care of Sean's business himself. He was generous like that. His announcement had the immediate effect of making Sean's face smooth from an annoyed and puzzled frown to his usual cheerful countenance. "That'd be grand. Let me know what you need from me."

"I will. There will likely be some paperwork."

"Any time, mate. Come into the pub, and we'll complete it over a glass of whiskey."

"I'll do that."

A much happier Sean O'Grady left, not even complaining about being brought here under false pretenses since we obviously weren't doing a launch for Giles Murray's book. I wondered if that book would even come out now. If he got any publicity, poor man, it was going to be of a very negative sort. But that wasn't my problem anymore.

"WELL, that wasn't a very dramatic denouement, was it?" a drawling voice said.

I'd had a pretty good idea that Oscar Wilde and Bartholomew Branson had been watching the drama from above. Sure enough, as soon as the last mortal had left, that acid-witted Victorian wandered in, tapping his walking stick on the stone floor.

Bartholomew Branson followed. "For once, I agree with that flamboyant windbag. If I'd been writing that scene, Quinn, a bomb would have gone off."

Oscar glanced at him with utter disdain. "To cover the sound of your appalling prose, I hope."

"Now look here—" Branson began, stabbing his finger toward his literary nemesis.

But I interrupted. I didn't have time for one of their petty squabbles. "I thought it was plenty dramatic enough. You mean because the detectives didn't arrest Giles Murray?"

"Even I have managed to watch enough of your tedious drawing room TV mysteries to understand that an arrest is the inevitable culmination of the search for a murderer." Oscar thought for a minute. "Unless, of course, the murderer is killed at the end. Neither of which happened today."

Lochlan moved to stand by my side, as though in moral support. "They may not know what they're going to arrest him for. But don't worry, DI Walsh will see justice done. He's a good man."

I also felt that I'd done a pretty good job. Frankly, my pride was wounded. I'd like to see Oscar Wilde interrogate a suspect until they cracked. The trouble with Oscar was he was so busy creating beautiful and ingenious soap bubbles out of words that he didn't always give room for anyone else to speak. Not that I was one to malign a literary legend but, like many famous people, he was interesting on the page and could be a pain in the butt in the flesh.

Oscar let out a huge sigh. "Well, after that lackluster farce,

I shall go out and see if I can find more stimulating entertainment."

"Maybe you can find the dead Oscar Wilde fan club," Bartholomew Branson said.

I didn't know if he was aware, but he was beginning to imitate Oscar Wilde's sneer pretty well. I had to hide my smile, or I would have encouraged him to continue.

I said, "You know, Oscar, it was you who helped me see the truth."

That stopped him in his tracks. He turned, looking surprised and, dare I say, gratified. "How so?"

I enjoyed this moment. I'll admit it. I enjoyed it *a lot*. So I let my pause lengthen before I said, "It was while I was reading *The Picture of Dorian Gray*. I started thinking about the way pictures can hide the reality of what's going on. I mean, let's face it, there was a story behind the story in every one of Giles Murray's pictures in his book. He curated them to leave out all the bits he didn't think were picturesque and heartwarmingly nostalgic about Ballydehag."

I had thought Oscar Wilde would be honored, but instead he gave another one of his long-suffering sighs. "I might have known my perfectly magnificent treatise on art and the aesthetic in the modern age would turn into nothing but a game of Cluedo to you people. If you've no more insults to hurl at my head, I'll be on my way."

Bartholomew looked hurt. "I'm the one who writes bestselling contemporary thrillers, Quinn. I would have thought I'd have helped solve your mystery."

Oh, no sooner had I smoothed one set of vampire feathers than here was another set ruffled for me to deal with. "You did, Bartholomew. I couldn't pick one book of yours that helped. Your whole body of work is about crime and punishment."

And thank goodness Oscar had left, so I didn't have to put up with his cutting comeback. Bartholomew bought it. His ego was such that it didn't need much help from me to blow it back up into its normal balloon-like proportions.

Much more cheerfully now, he said, "Well, I'll be on my way, too." And then as he neared the door, he turned back to say, "Good work, Quinn."

After he'd gone, I took the nearest chair and slumped into it. Without me even asking, Lochlan poured me a brandy. It was still a little fiery on my tongue, but at least it wasn't Irish whiskey.

Deirdre, who had been quietly standing on the sidelines listening to all of this, said, "But what I don't understand, Quinn, is how you figured it out? I've read *The Picture of Dorian Gray* too, and I never got to solve a murder. I just felt so sorry for poor Sybil Vane."

I said to Lochlan, "Can you send one of your vampires to my store to collect the box of books that Biddy O'Donnell tried to sell to me?"

He left the room for a minute. Soon I saw a young vampire who could have been any high-tech worker in any cubicle in any connected city in the world slip past us. Within minutes, he was back placing the box of books at my feet. We all gathered around.

I said, "That's it, isn't it? The key?"

Lochlan nodded. "I rather think you might be right."

Dierdre came over and looked into the box too. "I'm still in the dark," she said.

I started reading off the book titles. "I can't believe I didn't see it right away. *QB VII, The A.B.C. Murders, 1984*. Put all those letters and numbers together and you've got a key." To Dierdre, I explained that the key was a password for Glyn McTavish's crypto account.

Lochlan said, "Unfortunately, Giles Murray didn't take proper care to replace those books in the order Glyn McTavish had kept them."

"I know. I bet he'd even carefully packed those books in the boxes so that he would be certain that they were in the same order." I spun the box around and there was a number 1 written in pen on the side. "The boxes he disposed of must have been numbered, too." I felt like kicking something. "I feel so bad. Now that charity will never get its money back."

"You're not to worry, Quinn," Lochlan said. "They've had their money returned."

I felt a warmth around my heart. He was looking at me with an odd expression and I said, "You gave the money back yourself, didn't you?"

When he nodded, I stood up and threw my arms around him. He put me gently away from him, looking very uncomfortable.

"Quinn, you must understand. I've done terrible deeds. I have extraordinary wealth that I've accumulated simply by being alive for so long. It's a very small way to make amends."

Still, it mattered. His generosity mattered to me.

I said, "I suppose we could start working with all the books Glyn McTavish owned and maybe eventually, with enough combinations, we'd stumble on the right password."

"Quinn, that would be a life's work."

I was beginning to see the humor in the situation.

"Exactly. I thought if we gave Billy the Mouth the project, that might keep him out of trouble."

Lochlan threw back his head and laughed. "I've got computer programs that would run all the combinations in a matter of days, or hours more likely."

I tapped my forefinger on his shoulder. "And you will never tell Billy that such technology exists."

His eyes were still dancing as he nodded solemnly. "It's one way to keep that thug occupied."

I agreed. "Now we just have to figure out how to keep Biddy and Blood out of trouble. Oh yeah, and then there are the leprechauns."

He said, "I'm not sure we'll be seeing much more of them. The treasure didn't materialize. I expect they'll go on to greener pastures."

I very much hoped he was right.

However, when I opened my shop the next morning, the first person in was Paddy McGrath. I'd have expected him to drop by merely to bid me goodbye if he came at all, but he looked quite pleased with himself. He'd sewn the button back on his jacket, or his wife had, and he came in carrying a cardboard gift box.

If there wasn't a warning to beware of leprechauns bearing gifts, I felt there ought to be. I was immediately suspicious.

He put the box on my cash desk and said with a chuckle, "Don't look so horrified. I made these specially for you."

I went from being horrified to hopeful. Maybe his wife really could bake. Maybe inside was the best loaf of Irish soda bread I'd ever tasted. I didn't smell fresh baking, but still I was hopeful. I eased the lid off the box and stared.

Nestled inside a piece of white tissue paper was a pair of shoes. I took them out of the paper and set them on the counter. They looked like the shoes Paddy wore, with a chunky heel and a squared off toe, but instead of the gold buckle, he'd created a flower out of strips of leather. And he'd dyed the shoes green. They were brilliant. I'd not seen shoes nearly as nice as this on the fashion runways in London or Paris.

He watched me anxiously as I picked one up and turned it around in my hand. "What do you think?"

"Paddy, I think you're a genius."

He beamed at me. "It became apparent very quickly that running a bakery would only be another in a series of disasters. My wife's soda bread is good, I'll grant you, but it can be a little heavy. And her attempts at anything else have been less than successful. But the pair of us have been cobblers for a long time. I saw the shoes you had on the other day, and I thought, the style's come back around again. So, with a little experimentation, and watching a few runway shows—and their shoes—on YouTube, I got the idea."

"Can I try them on?" I was terribly worried they wouldn't fit.

As though he'd read my mind, he said, "I've a good eye for a foot size. I think they'll fit." And then he winked at me.

I was so pleased I was wearing a skirt today. I slipped off my boring black pumps and stepped into the shoes. To say they felt like magic would have been silly, but they were comfortable and the most perfect fit. I did a short runway strut up and down so Paddy could see them from every angle, and both of us were clearly delighted.

He said, "So that's what we've decided to do. I'm very

sorry you won't be getting fresh bread, but I'm going to convert the bakery into a proper cobbler's shop, where we'll not only repair shoes, but we'll design and make new ones."

"But what about the treasure?" I had to ask.

He shrugged, looking philosophical. "Perhaps luck really does favor the industrious."

I had to laugh. "Perhaps it does."

"I hope you'll wear these shoes, and if you feel inclined, perhaps you could tell your friends and even post about my shoes on Instagram."

The very idea of using Instagram ever again gave me a slight shiver, but I knew I would have to get over myself. I suggested that he might also want to make a pair for Karen Tate, and he twinkled at me.

"I already have. She's got so many visitors coming through that bed and breakfast of hers, I suspect they will help spread the word."

I was thinking fast. "You'll need a website."

"Aye, that I will. I was hoping you might talk to the owner of Devil's Keep. I've heard that Lochlan Balfour listens to you. Perhaps he'll even consider doing a launch of my line of shoes when they're ready."

I thought the chance that Lochlan Balfour was ever going to launch anything again at my instigation was on the none end of the slim-to-none scale. But I didn't want to dampen Paddy McGrath's spirits. Not quite yet. I was pretty sure Lochlan would help with the website and social media, and probably that was what Paddy McGrath really needed.

The leprechaun went off whistling, and I continued to admire my new shoes.

Unfortunately, my good mood was soon ruined. My next

visitors were Thomas Blood and Biddy O'Donnell, who slipped in as soon as Paddy McGrath left. Not even my beautiful new shoes could hold my positive mood as I contemplated these two thieves, connivers, and liars. I planted my hands on my hips and glared at the pair of them.

"And what do you want?"

Biddy took a step back, and her wobbly head jerked to the side. She reached up and slipped her head back into place. "If you've no more use for those books we brought along, missy, we'll be taking them off your hands."

I shook my head at her. "Oh no, you won't. I know where you got them. You caused a great deal of trouble and interfered in a police investigation."

They didn't look very worried. I supposed that me threatening a vampire and an ancient witch with modern-day police wasn't very terrifying. Biddy's crafty old eyes peered around the bookstore. "You're selling them yourself, aren't you? I'll remember this, Quinn Callahan. I'll remember you cutting out your own flesh and blood from this money-making venture."

"Oh no, I'm not. As you must know, they belong to the estate of the murdered man you stole them from."

She made a clicking noise with her remaining teeth. "It wasn't like he was going to be reading them, now was it?"

"No, but he did have a will. He left everything he had to a charity in New York. Those books will be auctioned off, and the money will go to help widows and orphans."

She made a disgusted noise at that. "What about me, then? Aren't I a widow? Twice over."

"Aye, that you are, sweet lady," Thomas Blood said, oozing sympathy.

"You're only a widow because you did away with your husbands," I reminded her.

"That was never proved," she said with dignity. Well, what dignity she had when her head wobbled off her neck again.

Thomas Blood, never one to waste time on a lost cause, said, "Come along, my dear, there's that auction in Cork that we wanted to get to."

He bent his arm and she put her hand in the crook of his elbow. They departed like an old-fashioned courting couple.

Good riddance.

Dierdre came in then and said, "Quinn, have you had any ideas about what we should read for this week's book club?"

I heaved a sigh that Oscar would have been proud of. "Dierdre, I don't care what it is, but please let it be a comedy."

Thanks for reading *A Poisonous Review!* I hope you enjoyed Quinn's adventure. While you're waiting for the next adventure of the Vampire Book Club, here's the beginning of *Peony Dreadful*, the first book in a new series about a magical flower shop in the Cotswolds. Enjoy!

Peony Dreadful, Chapter One

FLOWERS HAVE a language all of their own. So do witches.

Naturally, I keep my witchiness on the down low.

People in my small Cotswold village of Willow Waters are suspicious enough of me. I wasn't born here, you see. Worse,

I'm an American. By birth, anyway, though naturalized by marriage to an Englishman. My mother named me Peony, as that was her favorite flower. I suppose I should be happy she didn't prefer Delphiniums or Agapanthus.

The families here go back five or six generations. To say the community is close is an understatement. If you were an outsider, it took a long time to be accepted.

Willowers, as they call themselves, were very proud of defending their beautiful village from the slew of out-of-towners who raced to the Cotswolds to buy their second (or third) homes, driving up the house prices, and yakking up a storm in the usually sedate local pubs. I can't blame them. One of the reasons I liked it here so much was the peace and quiet, the abundance of natural beauty.

The villagers might, eventually, have accepted me had Jeremy lived. Sadly, he didn't. You're wondering if I did away with him after a nasty fight, I can tell you are, and you've only known me a few minutes. And my witchiness had nothing to do with it, if that's what you're thinking. No spells. No curses. Nada. But you can see how my young husband dying suddenly made my neighbors suspicious. It's a small-town thing.

The truth was, I loved Jeremy and was devastated when he was taken from me in a freak riding accident three years ago. He took a jump badly, was thrown off his horse, and broke his neck. One terrible miscalculation, and he was gone in an instant. There are spells and potions that can heal a lot of hurts and illnesses, but a broken neck is final. I've never felt more powerless. Losing him tore me in two.

So, here I was, a reasonably young woman of thirty-two, widowed. I no longer fit in with the upwardly mobile couples who talked about the FTSE like it was a favorite sports team. It's the UK stock market, to save you having to look it up, and when people talk about it, they call it the Footsie. As in football. As in soccer. They drank unpronounceable French wine, went for mini-breaks in Cornwall, Devon, or a quick jaunt to a European city, shopped at Waitrose, and wore a lot of Barbour and wellies. It was not a bad life, as you can tell. But it wasn't mine anymore.

The industrious among our friendship group worked in London and commuted. Or they had flats in London and came down to Willow Waters on weekends. Now most of those couples were having children. It seemed that every week a new announcement was made and suddenly there were babies everywhere I looked, and the village echoed with the oohs and ahhs of cooing admirers. Jeremy and I had been discussing would we or wouldn't we, but his fall put an end to that conversation.

Husbandless and childless, I no longer fit into their world. Honestly, I'd never really fit in. That part I didn't mind. It was Jeremy who had bound me to that group. Without him, I fell away like a badly-glued drawer handle.

When Jeremy died, did I think about leaving Willow Waters and going back to Maine? Of course, I did. But we had the village flower shop by then. Bewitching Blooms was my idea. I've always loved flowers and, when Jeremy was made redundant from his finance job in the City (that's London in Britspeak) and got a decent severance package, we decided to open a shop. He wanted a gift shop to fleece the constant stream of tourists who came to enjoy our picturesque village, thus filling it with traffic and tour buses and rendering it much less picturesque. I wanted a flower shop.

We compromised. Bewitching Blooms sold flowers and gift items. Our customers appreciated getting everything in one place, and we'd received lots of compliments. It made Jeremy and me extremely proud, which was worth more than making us rich. We could pay the bills, and that was enough for us.

Do we know each other well enough yet for me to tell you a secret? Let's suppose we do. But don't worry. This secret's nothing bad. It goes back to the language of flowers, a language documented even before Shakespeare's time. Rosemary for remembrance, pansies for thoughts, and all that. But plants do so much more than represent emotions. The right flowers, in the right combinations, are as powerful as any spell. Especially if they're gently helped along by an actual spell.

And so, when I did the arrangements for a wedding, I'd imbue the bride's bouquet and the groom's boutonniere with the kind of magic that gave them a propitious start to married life. When sending a bouquet to someone who was ill, I'd sometimes give a little strengthening boost to the blooms. A new baby? What new mother didn't need a little nurturing herself and a good night's sleep? For a funeral, I liked to offer comfort to the bereaved.

Naturally, I kept the added bonuses a secret, but people tended to order from me again and again. Not because they understood what I'd done, but because on a deeper, unconscious level, they recognized my flowers had helped them. The repeat customers were welcome, of course, but the real pleasure came from knowing that I was doing good in our village. What's the point of being a white witch if you can't share the love, right?

And so, on that auspicious bright Thursday in May, I opened my eyes, little realizing my life was about to change. No, that's not true. My cat, Blue, woke me. She's a pretty marmalade who appeared the day Jeremy died, confidently padding into my kitchen, where I was doubled over, weeping, while my thirty-seven-year-old husband lay dead in the local funeral home. I picked her up and buried my face in her fur. She let me, and I immediately knew she was destined to become my familiar.

We've been together ever since. I named her Blodeuwedd, who is the Welsh Goddess of Spring and Flowers. It's pronounced 'bluh DIE weth'—hence Blue for short, otherwise it's a bit of a mouthful when you're calling her for dindins.

She was acting strange—restless, meowing, and headbutting me awake. Normally, it took several back rubs for me to even get her down to breakfast.

"What is it?" I asked, but she only glared balefully, as if I should know.

I blinked a few times, but all I saw was my bedroom. I still slept in the room I'd shared with Jeremy. Only these days, instead of his gentle snoring, I was lulled to sleep by Blue's soothing purring. My alarm was set for 7 a.m. to give me enough time to get ready for work, but it was only 6:30 and still a little misty outside. I groaned and tried to roll over, but I was awake now and somehow knew Blue wouldn't let me fall back to sleep.

Blue wasn't the most energetic of familiars. In fact, she was on the lazier end of the scale. Other familiars talked to their witches, strengthened their spells, did their bidding. If given the choice between helping with my magic or lazing around in the sun on her favorite spot on the couch, she'd go for the couch every time. After Jeremy died, she'd been a great comfort cat, and she'd clearly chosen me for a reason.

As far as I'd been able to see, her familiar talents came in two flavors. First, she was an excellent early warning system. Like now, when she was acting peculiar. That usually meant something unpleasant was about to happen. Her second talent was more nebulous. She strengthened my magic. If I cast a spell and made sure she was within my circle, it would be faster-acting and more efficacious. A bit like overdrive on a car. Pretty impressive for a little marmalade, right?

So the fact that she was acting so peculiar suggested that I should keep my wits about me. No doubt something was up and now that I was, too, I'd soon find out what it was.

Peony Dreadful is book one of a brand new series of paranormal cozy mysteries you won't want to miss. Sign up for my newsletter at NancyWarrenAuthor.com to hear about all of my new releases.

A Note from Nancy

Dear Reader,

Thank you for reading *A Poisonous Review.* I am delighted to write about an older, more experienced witch and very happy to find so many readers are enjoying older characters. I hope you'll consider leaving a review and please tell your friends who like paranormal women's fiction and cozy mysteries. Review on Amazon, Goodreads or BookBub.

If you enjoy paranormal cozy mysteries, you might also enjoy *The Vampire Knitting Club* - a story that NYT Bestselling Author Jenn McKinlay calls "a delightful paranormal cozy mystery perfectly set in a knitting shop in Oxford, England. With intrepid, late blooming amateur sleuth, Lucy Swift, and a cast of truly unforgettable characters, this mystery delivers all the goods."

Join my newsletter for a free prequel, *Tangles and Treasons*, the exciting tale of how the gorgeous Rafe Crosyer, from *The Vampire Knitting Club* series, was turned into a vampire.

I hope to see you in my private Facebook Group. It's a lot of fun. www.facebook.com/groups/NancyWarrenKnitwits

Until next time,
Happy Reading,

Nancy

ALSO BY NANCY WARREN

The best way to keep up with new releases, plus enjoy bonus content and prizes is to join Nancy's newsletter at NancyWarrenAuthor.com or join her in her private Facebook group www.facebook.com/groups/NancyWarrenKnitwits

Village Flower Shop: Paranormal Cozy Mystery

Peony Dreadful - Book 1

Vampire Book Club: Paranormal Women's Fiction Cozy Mystery

Crossing the Lines - Prequel

The Vampire Book Club - Book 1

Chapter and Curse - Book 2

A Spelling Mistake - Book 3

A Poisonous Review - Book 4

Vampire Knitting Club: Paranormal Cozy Mystery

Tangles and Treasons - a free prequel for Nancy's newsletter subscribers

The Vampire Knitting Club - Book 1

Stitches and Witches - Book 2

Crochet and Cauldrons - Book 3

Stockings and Spells - Book 4

Purls and Potions - Book 5

Fair Isle and Fortunes - Book 6

Lace and Lies - Book 7

Bobbles and Broomsticks - Book 8

Popcorn and Poltergeists - Book 9

Garters and Gargoyles - Book 10

Diamonds and Daggers - Book 11

Herringbones and Hexes - Book 12

Ribbing and Runes - Book 13

Cat's Paws and Curses - A Holiday Whodunnit

Vampire Knitting Club Boxed Set: Books 1-3

Vampire Knitting Club Boxed Set: Books 4-6

Vampire Knitting Club Boxed Set: Books 7-9

The Great Witches Baking Show: Culinary Cozy Mystery

The Great Witches Baking Show - Book 1

Baker's Coven - Book 2

A Rolling Scone - Book 3

A Bundt Instrument - Book 4

Blood, Sweat and Tiers - Book 5

Crumbs and Misdemeanors - Book 6

A Cream of Passion - Book 7

Cakes and Pains - Book 8

Whisk and Reward - Book 9

Gingerdead House - A Holiday Whodunnit

The Great Witches Baking Show Boxed Set: Books 1-3

Abigail Dixon: A 1920s Cozy Historical Mystery

In 1920s Paris everything is très chic, except murder.

Death of a Flapper - Book 1

Toni Diamond Mysteries

Toni is a successful saleswoman for Lady Bianca Cosmetics in this series of humorous cozy mysteries.

Frosted Shadow - Book 1

Ultimate Concealer - Book 2

Midnight Shimmer - Book 3

A Diamond Choker For Christmas - A Holiday Whodunnit

Toni Diamond Mysteries Boxed Set: Books 1-4

The Almost Wives Club

An enchanted wedding dress is a matchmaker in this series of romantic comedies where five runaway brides find out who the best men really are!

The Almost Wives Club: Kate - Book 1

Secondhand Bride - Book 2

Bridesmaid for Hire - Book 3

The Wedding Flight - Book 4

If the Dress Fits - Book 5

The Almost Wives Club Boxed Set: Books 1-5

Take a Chance series

Meet the Chance family, a cobbled together family of eleven kids who are all grown up and finding their ways in life and love.

Chance Encounter - Prequel

Kiss a Girl in the Rain - Book 1

Iris in Bloom - Book 2

Blueprint for a Kiss - Book 3

Every Rose - Book 4

Love to Go - Book 5

The Sheriff's Sweet Surrender - Book 6

The Daisy Game - Book 7

Take a Chance Boxed Set: Prequel and Books 1-3

For a complete list of books, check out Nancy's website at NancyWarrenAuthor.com

ABOUT THE AUTHOR

Nancy Warren is the USA Today Bestselling author of more than 100 novels. She's originally from Vancouver, Canada, though she tends to wander and has lived in England, Italy and California at various times. While living in Oxford she dreamed up The Vampire Knitting Club. Favorite moments include being the answer to a crossword puzzle clue in Canada's National Post newspaper, being featured on the front page of the New York Times when her book Speed Dating launched Harlequin's NASCAR series, and being nominated three times for Romance Writers of America's RITA award. She has an MA in Creative Writing from Bath Spa University. She's an avid hiker, loves chocolate and most of all, loves to hear from readers!

The best way to stay in touch is to sign up for Nancy's newsletter at NancyWarrenAuthor.com or www.facebook.com/groups/NancyWarrenKnitwits

To learn more about Nancy and her books
NancyWarrenAuthor.com

facebook.com/AuthorNancyWarren
twitter.com/nancywarren1
instagram.com/nancywarrenauthor
amazon.com/Nancy-Warren/e/B001H6NM5Q
goodreads.com/nancywarren
bookbub.com/authors/nancy-warren

Printed in Great Britain
by Amazon